Courteous, courageous and commanding—
these heroes lay it all on the line for the
people they love in more than fifty stories about
loyalty, bravery and romance.
Don't miss a single one!

ALLISON LEIGH

SECRETLY MARRIED

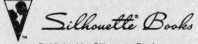

Published by Silhouette Books

America's Publisher of Contemporary Romance

 SILHOUETTE BOOKS

Recycling programs for this product may not exist in your area.

ISBN-13: 978-0-373-36277-6

SECRETLY MARRIED

Copyright © 2004 by Allison Lee Davidson

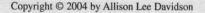

Printed in U.S.A.

ALLISON LEIGH

started early by writing a Halloween play that her grade-school class performed. Since then, though her tastes have changed, her love for reading has not. And her writing appetite simply grows more voracious by the day.

She has been a finalist for a RITA® Award and a Holt Medallion. But the true highlights of her day as a writer are when she receives word from a reader that they laughed, cried or lost a night of sleep while reading one of her books.

Born in Southern California, Allison has lived in several different cities in four different states. She has been, at one time or another, a cosmetologist, a computer programmer and a secretary. She has recently begun writing full-time after spending nearly a decade as an administrative assistant for a busy neighborhood church. She currently makes her home in Arizona with her family. She loves to hear from her readers, who can write to her at P.O. Box 40772, Mesa, AZ 85274-0772, or visit her Web site at www.allisonleigh.com.

For my family.

Prologue

The Moonlight Chapel of Love.

Delaney Townsend slid off her blazer and folded it over her arm. Even at two in the morning, the air in Vegas was hot. But it wasn't the heat that disturbed her, particularly. It was the entire situation in which she found herself.

"Something wrong?" The man standing with her grazed her bare arm with a long finger.

Despite herself, despite the heat, despite…everything…she shivered from the contact. She glanced up at Samson Vega if for no other reason than the sight of him was far more reassuring than the sight of the Moonlight Chapel of Love.

If she repeated the chapel's name often enough in her head, would some of the shock recede?

"It's…blinking," she finally said.

The corner of Sam's mouth kicked up, and her stomach clutched in the odd little way it had done since the very first time she'd seen that half smile of his.

If only she'd been stronger against that disarming appeal, they wouldn't be standing in front of a merrily blinking wedding chapel at two in the morning.

"It is pretty bright," he allowed blandly.

Understatement. She felt a bubble of laughter rising inside her. Or maybe it was hysteria. "There's a line of people waiting."

He nodded, though his gaze was on her rather than the couples waiting outside the shiny white-and-gold double doors. She'd long ago given up the idea that his manner of focusing on a person was because of his profession. It wasn't cop. It was simply *him*. Undiluted.

And it was lethal to a woman's common sense.

"Well." Delaney's voice was faint. It had a tendency to get that way when he looked at her like that. As if he couldn't wait to feast.

On her.

His lips curved slowly. Sam tucked his hand around her arm, his thumb dragging in a slow circle over the inside of her elbow. "Line isn't going to get any shorter."

The truth of which was proved by an impossibly young boy and girl who climbed from the rear of an ungodly long limousine that stopped at the curb. They ran—arms entangled, laughter spilling—across the brief grassy area to take a place at the end of the line.

She barely had a chance to realize that she, at the

grand old age of thirty-four, felt old at the sight of their youthful enthusiasm when the shining double doors opened wide and a couple stepped from inside the chapel. Silly smiles lit their faces, and even from this distance she could see the gold bands on their fingers.

"They look like they belong on the top of a wedding cake." She hadn't realized people would dress in full wedding regalia to visit a place like…this.

"Is that what you wanted? The whole wedding getup?"

She realized she was watching the emerging couple with the sort of morbid fascination usually reserved for vehicular accidents. "No."

Sam chuckled softly, his head angling toward her. "Don't sound so horrified. We could still do this back home, you know. You wouldn't even have to dress up like a Barbie-gone-berserk in ruffles and lace. If you want your mother or your dad—"

"No." She was acting like a ninny. There was no other word for it. She'd agreed to marry him, and they both wanted to do it *now,* so it was ridiculous to act as if she was rethinking the decision. "The last thing we need is to have my mother and my father cooped together even for the ten-minute duration of a ceremony. We'd *all* live to regret it."

"Do you regret this?"

Delaney's breath caught a little. "You do believe in being direct, don't you."

His right eyebrow rose a fraction. "You ought to know." His tone was low. Intimate. "Usually makes things easier in the long run."

And she usually agreed. But logic wasn't ruling her these days; it had been shoved aside in favor of the madness created by letting him into her life during a weak moment.

She watched the departing cake-topper couple for a moment. He wanted to marry her. In all the time she'd known Sam, she'd never known him to prevaricate.

The direct approach.

Her stomach swam.

"Hey." He turned her to face him, nudging a thumb under her chin. "I know how to warm up cold feet."

"That's what got us here." Her voice was tart, but Delaney still found herself leaning into him.

"Don't hear me complaining." His mouth covered hers in a slow brush, and she felt the curve of that kicked-up corner. "So, are you ready?" She felt his words on her lips, too. Then his hand slid behind her neck. Something so simple. The touch of a man's warm palm, the gentle press of long, blunt-tipped fingers, the soft heat of masculine lips.

Only it wasn't simple at all. Because she'd shared kisses before with perfectly attractive, interesting men. None of them had made her knees weak. Until this man, who'd been complicating her life from the moment they'd met two years ago. First professionally. Then personally.

Her better sense knew that marrying him was akin to jumping from the frying pan into the fire. But then he lifted his head, his deep brown eyes focused only on her…*her*…and her heartbeat skittered. She stopped listening to common sense and followed her heart.

"Yes," she whispered back. "I'm ready."

Sam's smile was slow and all the more sweet because of it. He slid his hand down her arm, finding her hand. Slipped his fingers between hers, palm meeting palm.

They walked over and joined the end of the line.

One hour later, after a service that lasted all of seven minutes, Delaney Townsend and Samson Vega emerged from the shining white double doors, silly smiles on their faces and gold wedding bands on their ring fingers.

Chapter 1

Two years.

The first time since she'd seen Sam in two years, and he was in the arms of another woman.

Not just some witness he was questioning after a crime. Not some elderly woman he was helping to cross the street. It was clichéd, but she'd watched him do that, more than once, as if he were "good guy" personified.

No, *this* woman with whom he danced was definitely not elderly, and if she were witnessing anything, it was what it felt like to press her temple against Sam's strong jaw while they swayed together beneath a starlit sky.

Well, wasn't this just dandy?

Delaney exhaled and paused at the fringe of the crowd spilling from the clearing that was being used as a dance floor. Despite the outdoor setting, she felt hemmed in by too-warm bodies, too-loud music.

And Sam.

She hadn't let herself think too deeply about how she'd feel seeing him again after all this time. Silly, considering that she was a psychiatrist. Now, like a tongue gingerly approaching a suspect tooth, she probed not only at what she felt seeing Sam, but what she felt seeing him dance closely with another woman.

Tiny red, blue and green lights were strung from the tops of young trees, circling bushes, sprouting from the swaying fronds of palm trees, even though the holiday season was half a year away. They blinked and twinkled, casting the revelers in a surrealistic light.

That's what it felt like, Delaney decided.

Surreal.

How had their lives come to this?

The question was moot. She knew good and well how.

She glanced over at the main building that loomed against the studded sky. Fortunately, young Alonso was taken care of and was now settled in at the halfway house, Castillo House. She'd said her goodbye, difficult as it had been. Which meant that all Delaney had left to accomplish was this one last…task.

Maybe it was foolish. But to leave without at least speaking with him smacked of cowardice. It might appear that she was still affected by what had happened. And she didn't want him thinking that way. Even if it were true.

She exhaled again, smoothed first the front of her regrettably wrinkled suit, then the strands of hair that kept slipping free of the pins, and headed into the fray of dancers.

She turned this way and that, moving between and around couples, murmuring an apology when she bumped right into one couple while avoiding another. But her voice was absorbed by the music blaring from the sound system just as surely as the high heels of her pumps sank into the earth, and she was fairly certain that nobody paid any heed at all to her progress through the melee.

That was okay. Having the element of surprise on her side could only be a good thing where Sam was concerned. She was prepared, while he was not. He couldn't possibly be. A cowardly approach, perhaps, but there you have it.

She sidestepped, avoiding a couple intent on an enthusiastically bad tango, and finally came face-to-face with Sam.

Well, face to back.

She willed away a foolish surge of nervousness. For heaven's sake, surely she was past the stage of butterflies where he was concerned.

She cleared her throat a little. "Excuse me." Her voice was swallowed whole by the swell of the female singer and a symphony orchestra. She sighed a little and tried again, shifting when Sam and his partner slowly revolved and Delaney found herself standing behind the other woman. "*Excuse* me." She tapped the dark-haired woman's arm.

Immediately the woman looked around, her eyebrows lifting as she looked over her shoulder.

Sam noticed her then, too. His gaze narrowed on her face, his eyebrows jerking for a moment before drawing together over his hawkish nose. All around their odd little trio, the dancers continued to sway.

Well. She *had* managed to surprise him. Who knew? "Sorry to interrupt," she said smoothly. "I just wanted a moment of your time."

The woman's head swiveled from Delaney to Sam and back again, and Delaney stuck out her hand, feeling some sympathy for the bemused-looking woman who shook it. "Delaney…Townsend." She hesitated over the name. She'd have to work on that. She'd only been using it since she'd been in contact with Castillo House— two months, now, when she should have begun using it two years ago.

"Sara Drake," the other woman murmured.

"Drake?" Delaney looked over at the enormous mission-style house that provided a backdrop along with the trees and lights. "Are you related to Logan Drake?"

"He's my brother," Sara confirmed. "But I'm afraid I don't—"

"What the hell are you doing here, Delaney?" Sam interrupted the exchange.

Meeting his gaze was more difficult than she'd expected. So she looked at the total picture of him. The shining black hair springing back from his forehead, as thick as ever. Why couldn't the man at least have a receding hairline? Or a paunch instead of a body that looked—as impossible as it ought to be—even harder and stronger than before.

Before.

Which reminded her of the task currently at hand.

She tightened her grip on the strap of her briefcase. She had to raise her voice more than she was comfortable with to be heard above the music. "I'd just like to speak with you. It'll only take a minute, and you can get back to your dance partner." She managed a smile at Sara and felt relatively certain that it was harmlessly noncommittal. Butterflies or not, after having spent most of the day traveling—with the final hour spent sitting on a cold, wet seat in a boat that stank of gas and oil fumes—she suddenly felt rather more like baring her teeth at Sam.

Which would have shocked all of them, no doubt. Particularly Sam, since he'd considered her singularly unemotional when it came to certain matters.

She pushed a little more cheer into her smile. "Just a few minutes or less of your time, Sam. That's all I want."

"Townsend," Sam said abruptly.

She gave up trying to smile altogether. She'd come to the island of Turnabout for reasons that had nothing to do with him. But her reason for wanting to speak privately was solely due to his stubbornness. That didn't mean she wanted to create a scene right there in front of God and country and the dancers celebrating the anniversary of Castillo House's opening. "This is hardly the place to—"

"Why not? You're the one who's here."

The other woman, Sara, was looking decidedly uncomfortable. "I'm sorry," Delaney told her. She was.

She really had no desire to cause anyone discomfort. If she did, she could just hand over the box right now. Maybe Sam would turn around and present it to Sara.

The idea was nauseating.

"Perhaps somewhere more private is a good idea," Sara said softly, and the look Sam gave the woman— as if he were actually weighing her suggestion—gave Delaney a pang that she shouldn't have felt.

There was no need for Delaney to gingerly probe her feelings now. Not with the way her stomach suddenly churned. She quickly slid a bulging manila envelope from her briefcase. "Two minutes, Sam. That's all I'm asking."

"Is it?" He looked down at the envelope, lips thinning. "Don't think so."

She had a ridiculous urge to stomp her foot. And since she'd never been the foot-stomping sort she squelched it. "It's been two y—"

"Twenty-one months."

Delaney's words dried. She looked down at the envelope and pressed her palm against the buttons of her suit jacket, cursing the way her stomach rocked. Right. Twenty-one months. She could have even more accurately calculated the last time they'd seen each other down to days but didn't want to give him the satisfaction.

The night temperature seemed to have risen. Which was ridiculous. It had to be her. Becoming hot under the collar. Literally. If only she'd thought to wear a blouse, a camisole, something more substantial than a bra beneath her jacket. She could have removed the jacket, then, in deference to the heat. She'd checked the weather before making the trip to California and thought she'd been prepared for the warmer climate. So much for that notion.

"Why don't I get you some punch," Sara suggested suddenly. Too perceptively. "You and Sam can find a quiet place to talk." She smiled, doing a better job of it than Delaney had. "Take care of your business."

They were all adults. It didn't bother Delaney at all that it apparently took urging from Sara before Sam would be cooperative.

Right.

She exhaled and surreptitiously tugged at the front of her jacket in hopes of getting some air. "Punch would be nice," she lied. If she tried to swallow anything but water, she wasn't sure she could be responsible for the consequences.

Sam lifted a sardonic brow when Delaney hesitated as Sara moved away. "Well?"

She followed.

The woman—taller than Delaney by several inches—seemed to have far less difficulty making her way through the crowd. Or maybe people just naturally got out of Sara's way in the same manner they did for Sam.

Delaney watched the pair of them from the corner of her eyes. Sam and Sara. A striking couple. Both tall and raven-haired. They could have been brother and sister, only, Delaney knew Sam had no sister named Sara. Janie, yes. But not Sara.

Not that she'd ever met Janie, or his brother, Leo.

Not that she ever would.

The envelope crinkled as her fingers tightened. She

nearly jumped out of her skin when Sam closed his hand around her elbow.

"Little jumpy, Delaney?"

He used to call her Laney. She carefully moved her arm away from his touch. "It's been a long day," she said smoothly. It was the gospel truth. An incredibly long day. But it was worth it to have Alonso taken care of. She'd worked long and hard to make sure of it.

"Delaney." Sam watched her much too closely. "You all right?"

He'd recovered from his surprise. Now she couldn't read his expression to save her soul. A regrettably familiar position.

She lifted an eyebrow and brushed a strand of hair away from her face again. "Right as rain, Sam." But her voice was clipped despite herself and she deliberately looked around. Sara had made it to the row of tables near the house, laden with food and refreshments. But Sam and Delaney were still amidst the dancers and had finally begun to draw attention. "Is it serious between you two?" She cringed at that. *Don't ask the question if you're not prepared to listen to the answer.*

"Does it bother you to think it might be?"

"Is it still impossible for you to give a straight answer?"

"What do you think?"

"I think you're as annoying now as you ever were," she said evenly. She turned on her heel, grateful to keep her balance with her sinking heels. She should have just given him the ring, whether it embarrassed him or not, and gone on her way. Or, better yet, she should have left it with Annie and Logan Drake. They could have de-livered it. He would hardly have refused that type of personal delivery.

There were just too many "should haves" where Sam was concerned.

She realized Sam hadn't moved, and turned around to look, only to find him looking right back at her, his head cocked to one side. Studying? Judging?

Then he suddenly turned his head and Delaney followed suit, looking over to the house.

Alonso slouched against the wall near the high, double-wide door, his hands shoved in the pockets of the new baggy jeans she'd given him. His stance was casual, but Delaney knew it was feigned.

Even though Delaney had prepared herself for this, too, she still felt herself bracing. Still felt defiance coursing through her, joining the rock 'n' roll beat inside her stomach.

Sam looked back at her.

Oh, yes. Definitely judging.

Her grip tightened on the envelope as Sam headed toward her, his steps unhurried. He stopped just in front of her. "Should have known this would have something to do with him," he said, angling his head so she could hear his low voice. "Some things never change."

Her throat went tight. "Some people never change, either." He wasn't expressionless, she realized. An angry muscle flexed in his tight jaw.

"When are you going to learn your lesson where he's concerned? Hasn't he cost you enough?"

You mean when he cost me *you?* She wanted to voice the question. Better sense prevented her. "He has a name, Sam. Alonso. And *he's* cost me nothing of value." Her voice was flat. Hopefully it disguised the pain.

He tilted his head again, considering. "Been practicing your target shooting, I see."

"Alonso has been accepted as a resident at Castillo House. You might as well get used to seeing him on the island."

"In my jail cell, maybe."

Every nerve inside her tightened. The work Logan Drake and his wife, Annie, had accomplished in the past year at Castillo House with homeless and troubled youth had drawn attention from Delaney and her colleagues—enough attention that she'd swallowed the fact the program was located on Sam's turf and approached them about Alonso.

And Castillo House was Alonso's last chance to avoid jail time. The judge was out of patience where the boy's probation was concerned.

"Not without cause, Samson. Even you don't stoop that low, do you?"

Despite the music, the chatter, the revelry all around them, the silence between the two of them lengthened, thickened. "Crediting me with *some* integrity?" he finally asked. "There's a change."

She exhaled slowly, reining in a wealth of frustration and other emotions she didn't even want to put a name to. "Here." She pushed the envelope that contained the delicate wedding ring at him. "I don't know why you marked the envelope 'return to sender' in the first place. What kind of game you're—"

"It was never a game with you. A game would have been fun. Enjoyable."

The sentiment was nothing she hadn't already known. It still hurt.

"Then I'd think you'd be heartily glad to have this back." She wriggled the envelope, wishing he'd just take the thing.

"What's got you so anxious all of a sudden?"

She raised her eyebrows. "Sudden? I've tried sending this to you more than once!" She'd even tried a courier, to no avail.

"Maybe you should've taken the hint."

"What hint? That you want no reminders of our time together? I'm sure you don't. But the ring is—"

"Yours," he said flatly. "Even if you are doing something official now."

She blinked at that. "What's that supposed to mean?"

His head lowered another inch toward her and she steeled herself not to shift away. "Why now, Delaney?"

There was a burning deep behind her eyes. Her foot slid back. She shifted and glanced past him. Sara approached, bearing two plastic cups, filled to the brim, no doubt, with punch. "You're not the only one who's moving on, Sam." Some were just better at it than others.

His lips twisted. "Anyone I know?"

"Is it any of your business?"

"I think so." The envelope crinkled in his grip. "But let me guess. Your esteemed associate, Chadly Do-Wright."

Sam had never liked Chad Wright. Of course the reverse could be said, too. Chad had never particularly cared for Sam. If she'd known how things would end, she'd have paid more heed to Chad's sensible arguments from the start. Instead, she'd followed her heart.

Sam suddenly reached out, drawing the lock of hair away from her face. She stiffened her knees.

Not even her heart, she mentally corrected. She'd followed something far more base where Sam was concerned.

And people thought only *men* were ruled by lust. Now that was a serious joke.

As if he'd read her thoughts, he slipped his fingers along the strand of hair again. His knuckles brushed her temple. Her cheek.

"Don't touch me."

"Afraid Do-Wright wouldn't approve?" His fingertips slowly grazed the circle of her ear, taking extraordinary care in tucking the hair behind it.

"It's *Chad*." Her voice stalled altogether when his fingers glided along her jaw, and his thumb tucked beneath her chin, inexorably forcing it upward. She closed her eyes, then dragged her lids upward again, afraid of betraying any additional weakness.

She heard his tsk, even though it was half under his breath. "Look at you. As trussed-up as ever. At least, you're trying to be. Double-breasted suit. Hair in a knot. Only, you want to unbutton the suit, don't you. And your hair's falling down. Has Chad seen this side of you?"

"The crossing was windy."

His thumb slid over her lips, pressing them closed. "Ninety minutes on the open water. It usually is windy."

"Sam," her lips moved against the callused pad of his thumb. "The ring—"

"Screw the ring," he said flatly. Then his thumb moved and his head lowered. His mouth covered hers, inhaling the gasp of shock she couldn't prevent. His hand went behind her neck, preventing her from jumping back.

There was no love in the kiss. She knew it. He knew it.

He was angry. Twenty-one months hadn't seemed to change that fact one bit.

And he still tasted like the darkest, sweetest sin to ever exist as the kiss went on and on. Her body burned as she helplessly kissed him back.

She swayed when he finally let her free. Delaney was barely aware of the shock on Sara's face, or the stares of everyone else around them. She wanted to slap him. Kick him.

"That was uncalled for," she said hoarsely. "Absolutely."

"You're kidding, right?" His lips stretched in a humorless smile, and he suddenly turned around, facing the gaping onlookers.

His voice rose, so everyone could hear. "My wife, Delaney, finally comes to Turnabout, the least I can do is greet her with a kiss. Wouldn't you all agree?"

Chapter 2

*M*y wife.

Some deep instinct made Delaney lock her knees as Sam's comment rang in the sudden silence. If she'd had any doubt that Sam ever told anyone from Turnabout, his hometown, about their excruciatingly brief fiasco of a marriage, the shocked faces all around them removed it.

He'd turned back to her and was looking at her mouth. Despite the audience and her desire to tear out her hair and scream at him for this game he was playing, her lips tingled all over again.

And it was irritation at that, that got her moving again. She slapped the envelope against his chest. "You know we're no longer married," she snapped softly.

He exhaled sharply, turned and strode away.

The envelope fell.

She very nearly followed after him. He hadn't wanted to talk with her when they were married, why on earth would he want to when they weren't? If he wanted to walk away from what *should* have been a simple matter, she wasn't going to stop him.

He'd walked away from her before, after all.

She snatched up the envelope and headed blindly away from the curious eyes that seemed to be burning into her from all sides. But escape was blocked by the dancers one way and the whitewashed stucco building on the other. She trembled, never feeling more like screaming in her entire life.

Wouldn't that be a tidy item to add to her record? "After installing patient in residential program, subject became hysterical when former spouse referred to her as his wife...."

"Yo, Doc V. You didn't tell me Mr. Cop-man was gonna be here."

She marshaled her scrambled thoughts. Smoothed back her hair again and looked up at Alonso, who'd come down from his slouch to stand in front of her. He'd grown a foot in the past year. At only fifteen, he easily topped six feet, a good six inches taller than she. He was more gangly than broad, but she knew time would eventually fill in the spare gaps and he'd cut an impressive figure. "You being at Castillo House has nothing to do with Sam."

Alonso's lip curled. "Right."

Her day really had been too long. "Think about it."

Her tone was short enough that Alonso kept his next smart-aleck remark from emerging.

"Is he a cop here, too?" He focused on shoving up the long sleeves of his oversize T-shirt.

"He's the sheriff."

"Yeah, well he better not be hauling me off to jail, or—"

"Or?" Delaney looked sternly up into his young face. Alonso Petrofski was a combination of beauty from the mocha skin to the green eyes he'd inherited from his Jamaican mother and Russian father. In most respects, he was brilliant. And in most respects, troubled, neglected and full of anger and opinions. She'd started out as his court-appointed therapist. Now, a very rocky four years later, she'd like to think she was his friend.

Some days that was easier to believe than others.

"You're not going to jail, Alonso. Not unless you do something illegal here. And if you do that in the next two months, your probation will be revoked and you'll finish out your full sentence in jail back in New York. Then all the good work you've done the past year will be for nothing."

"Not if you can't find me," he said.

"Turnabout is an island, Alonso. You won't be going anywhere that we don't know about." Logan Drake, the man responsible for the running of Castillo House, smiled coolly, seeming to appear at their sides out of nowhere.

Alonso had already told Delaney he figured Logan was a hard-ass. Given what Delaney knew about Logan's former profession, she figured the assessment was fairly accurate.

"He's not exaggerating." A very pregnant girl stood beside Logan, addressing Alonso. "It's Drake's way or the highway. But believe me. He's easier than the sheriff. I've been here for three months, so I oughta know." She shot a rueful glance up at Logan, who softened a little and tugged the end of her long red braid.

"This is Caitlin Reed," Logan introduced. "She'll show you what chores you're assigned to tonight."

"Man, I just got here."

Delaney remained mum. This was Logan and Annie's center. The sooner Alonso became acclimated to his new home, the better.

Logan merely lifted one broad shoulder, his blue gaze again impassive. "Everybody here works, Alonso. You want to stay, you're welcome. But you're gonna work the same as the rest."

The boy stared Logan down for a long, taut minute. Alonso drew up every centimeter of height he possessed, as if it would give him some advantage against the man with whom he stood eye to eye. It had no effect on Logan. He merely waited. Solid. Strong. Sure. Then Alonso made an impatient sound, swore—under his breath, because swearing was against the rules of the house—and headed back up the shallow steps and inside the massive doorway. Delaney watched him go. Saw the way he curtailed his long-legged stride to accommodate Caitlin's shorter, somewhat waddling one.

Along with relief was a sense of loss. Alonso had

become a large part of her life. Right or wrong, he was more than a patient to her. But she couldn't handle him alone, and *something* had to be done. He was too young to be left to his own devices. He needed a home.

Hopefully, Castillo House would provide what she couldn't.

She glanced up at Logan. He hadn't said a word about Sam's outrageous announcement after kissing her, and she was grateful. "I know you don't really have room for him, yet, with your renovations still underway. But I appreciate it. He really needed to get away from his usual crowd."

"Long as your boy toes the line, we'll get along fine," Logan said. Then his hard face softened, making him look immeasurably younger, when a slender woman with a mass of blond curls stopped next to him, sliding her arm through his. Annie Drake.

"Alonso will be fine." Annie smiled far more easily than did her husband. "And we do appreciate the—"

Delaney waved away the thanks before Annie could finish. She didn't want to advertise the donation she'd arranged for Castillo House. "We can keep that between us." What her mother had donated would go a little way toward the renovations the big old house still required. A little way toward making the physical space necessary for another person. Like Alonso. Which made having to approach her mother for funds worth it. Just because Delaney had loathed having to do so, her mother's donation had been just one more in a long line of charitable causes she thoughtlessly supported, meaning nothing more nor less than if Delaney had been a stranger.

"Secrets have a way of coming out, Delaney. Sometimes it's better all around to put everything out on the table."

Delaney didn't know if that was a reference to her and Sam's history, or not. But there was nothing in Annie's expression that Delaney could take exception to.

She was just feeling defensive.

Because of Sam.

"Um, you're…Delaney. Right?"

A young woman had approached. Why not? For all the attention Sam had thrown her way, she might have been the circus come to town. "Yes."

"I'm Janie Vega."

Something indefinable curled through Delaney. So she'd meet some of Sam's family after all. "You're Sam's sister." Timid, she thought, as she looked for some resemblance between the girl and Sam. They had the same dark eyes, but that seemed to be all. "He told me about you."

"I wish we could say the same about you."

Maybe not so timid, after all, Delaney thought, eyeing Janie's crossed arms. Logan and Annie murmured excuses and moved off with no small amount of haste. "I'm sorry," she told Janie.

"Why? Sam's the one who's been keeping his mouth shut all this time." Her voice was tart. "Ironic, considering how he feels about deception."

Could this get any worse? Sam should have been the

one to soothe his sister's hurt feelings. "Well, really, Sam and I, we weren't together very long. And it *was* a few years ago."

"But," Janie's expression faltered a little, "he said you are his wife."

"*Was*," Delaney assured gently.

"You're more forgiving than I am if you think that's an adequate excuse for his behavior."

There was nothing suitable or otherwise that Delaney could say. Janie seemed to realize it. "Where are you staying tonight?" she asked.

The trip to Turnabout had taken longer than Delaney expected. Their flight from New York had been late arriving in San Diego, which meant they'd missed the regular ferry that ran twice a day. She'd had to hire a charter. Which was definitely a glorified term for the rough-riding bucket that had carried her and Alonso from the mainland to the tiny island of Turnabout.

She'd strongly entertained the idea of waiting until morning before finishing the journey. But her desire to get it over with had overridden her common sense. It would've been smarter to wait. Then she'd have been assured of a way off the island.

Now, she had a hotel room all reserved in San Diego that was going begging. "I hadn't planned to stay on Turnabout," she admitted. She didn't enjoy being caught unprepared. "Is there a hotel here?"

"Maisy Fielding has an inn. Called Maisy's Place. She has several guest cottages, too. But she's full up. I help out there when she's particularly busy." Janie lifted an arm, encompassing the crowd. "A lot of people came over to celebrate the first anniversary of Castillo House. But Sam has an extra room," Janie continued. "Etta does, too, but my father is using it now that he's home again."

"Etta?"

"Our grandmother. Henrietta Vega."

"Right." Surreal, indeed. Delaney looked around at the partyers. She was aware of Janie watching her closely.

It felt as if everyone was watching her closely. Too closely. She much preferred to focus her attention on others than to have that focus turned the other way around.

Sam had an extra room. Delaney wasn't so much interested in that as she was interested in what had possessed Sam to say the words he had.

My wife.

What purpose had that served? None. And she wanted to tell him so. She wanted him to understand—fully and completely—that she was no basket case. That she was moving on, just as she'd told him. Thoughtfully, intelligently, dispassionately. What she wanted now were common interests, common goals, a common purpose.

Things she and Sam had never had.

Except in bed.

She ignored the taunting whisper inside her head. The bedroom could break a relationship, but it was rare when it could make one. She and Sam were no exception to that.

"Perhaps you could tell me how to get to his house," she suggested. She'd tell him what she thought of his little "act" and she'd leave the ring. Once and for all, end of story.

Janie looked clearly relieved. "It's on the other end of the island, actually. I'll get Leo's cart and drive you over."

"Cart?"

"His golf cart. I don't have a car. Most of us don't. But it's a long walk from here to there."

Delaney rubbed her forehead. She didn't have a car, either. Because she lived in the city. *The* city. The big apple. Born and raised.

"Delaney? Ready?" Janie was eyeing her.

Oh, Delaney was too tired. She nodded. She'd have agreed to just about anything to get away from the curious stares she was still getting.

The golf cart sat outside the high iron fence that surrounded the Castillo House property. Delaney climbed onto the narrow front seat and grabbed on with a death grip when it lurched forward. Janie buzzed down the bumpy road, seemingly unconcerned by the absolute and utter darkness as they left behind the lights of the party.

No matter how dark, the rush of wind through the open cart still felt heavenly against Delaney's heated skin.

When Janie finally slowed the cart to a halt, it was in front of a sprawling, darkened house. "It doesn't look like your brother is here." Probably avoiding her, if for no other reason than to annoy her. He'd always been exceptionally adept in that area.

"Doesn't matter," Janie assured as they headed up the stone walk. "It's probably not locked. But even if it is, I have a key. I take care of his plants whenever he goes to the mainland."

Sam had plants?

With no hesitation, Janie pushed open the door. "See? Come on in." She waited in the darkened entrance.

Delaney stepped inside, vaguely aware of holding her breath. The memory of the tiny apartment Sam had lived in before they'd become involved flashed through her mind. It had possessed only the essentials. A bed. A fridge. A dim, cold bathroom. The place had practically been sterile, giving no hint whatsoever of the man who'd occupied it.

Janie flicked a switch, and light streamed downward from deceptively simple iron wall sconces.

She couldn't help her inhalation of surprise at her first impression of the interior. "Oh. My."

"Nice, isn't it?" Janie seemed to be looking at her with some kind of expectation.

"Yes." She smiled weakly. It was nice. Natural stone. A bronze wall that dripped with the soothing, unexpected sound of water. Plants. Leather furnishings. Nubby rugs over slate. It was full of thriving plants. Palms in the corners. A fern on a small table. It was modern. It was timeless.

It was…Sam?

She felt like rubbing her eyes. She refrained. Coming here had been a mistake. "I should wait for Sam somewhere else."

"Don't be ridiculous. You're his wife."

"Was. I *was* his wife. And as soon as I have a chance to speak with Sam, I'll be going."

Janie looked doubtful. "If you say so. Would have

been nice to get to know the woman who stole my big brother's heart, though."

"When you meet her, give her my regards." Silence met her response, and she sighed. Janie had done nothing to earn her sarcastic humor. "Sorry."

"I think this situation is odd for everyone." Given the circumstances, there was a surprising lack of judgment in Janie's voice as she headed into the house, flipping on more light switches as she went. When she came to the kitchen, though, she stopped. "You can wait for Sam here. Make yourself at home. I doubt he will be gone for too long."

If she were strictly honest with herself, Delaney wasn't sure if that was a comforting thought, or not. "Thanks, Janie."

The young woman gave a little sketch of a wave then disappeared up the hallway.

A moment later Delaney heard the soft, solid sound of the door closing.

She was alone in Sam's house.

My wife.

She exhaled shakily, pushing the thought away, and dumped her briefcase on the counter, her gaze skipping around the well-appointed kitchen. The only sound she could hear was water. The soft trickle from the water wall in the living room underscored by a low, constant murmur. It was the same sound of the ocean she'd heard when she and Alonso had been left at the dock by the charter boat.

Sighing again, she stepped out of her high heels,

leaving them sitting on the floor next to the granite counter, and unbuttoned her double-breasted jacket, waving it open a few times. Ah. Heaven.

She'd brought a change of clothes in her briefcase—slacks and a tunic—but it was so late there seemed little point in changing into them when they wouldn't be any cooler than her suit.

Still, she felt better just from the small respite, and she buttoned up again, then moved around the island toward the bank of windows lining the wall. Now, with the light on inside, they were more like mirrors that reflected her bedraggled appearance.

She slowly walked along them until she came to one that was a door. Cleverly designed, it barely differed from the oversize windows. She reached for the handle.

"I wouldn't go out there without the light. The cliff is closer than you think."

She snatched back her hand, whirling around. Sam stood next to the counter where she'd left her briefcase. The tails of his dark gray shirt were pulled from the black jeans he wore, and he'd rolled the sleeves farther up his forearms. His jaw was shadowed as it always had been by this time of night. He'd been a two-shave-a-day man.

Definitely thoughts she needed to avoid.

"I didn't know you were here," she said, stating the obvious, and felt stupid because of it.

"Passed Janie on my way in. Should have known her soft little heart couldn't withstand you."

Meaning *she* had no soft heart at all? "Your sister's the one who suggested I come here. Not me. But since you're back, I'll just leave this—" in two steps she'd snatched the envelope from the outer pocket of her briefcase and set it on the counter "—here and I'll go."

"How do you propose to do that? Whistle for a cab?" He flicked open another button at his neck. Energy seemed to vibrate from him, yet he was uncommonly still.

Even rattlesnakes possessed rattles as a warning device. Not Sam. His strike had always been unexpected. Never physical, but indelibly felt all the same. "Why does it matter to you how I leave? I just wanted to make sure you got the ring back."

"Yeah, I picked up on that."

She lifted her gaze, meeting his despite her intention otherwise. "And?"

"And I'm curious what you think you're doing."

Count to ten, Laney. Her voice was calm when she finally spoke. "What *I'm* doing? You're the one who told all those people that I was your wife."

"You are."

"Was, Sam. *Was.* You'll surely remember the small matter of our divorce!"

His head cocked a little, his gaze measuring. "Have you taken to drink, Delaney?"

Her fingers curled. Uncurled. "Don't be obtuse." Her brother had been the drinker in her family. "And while it pains me no end to have to ask, would you give me a ride back to Castillo House?"

"Why?"

"Because I need a place to sleep! And I'd rather

impose on Logan and Annie Drake for a corner on a floor somewhere than spend another minute with you."

"Go for it. Those fancy shoes lying there are gonna get beat to hell walking all the way, but—"

Her hands curled. "You won't even give me a ride?"

"Considering how nicely you've asked?" He snorted softly and reached out one long arm to hook open a drawer. "Here." He tossed her the small flashlight he withdrew. "You might need that. No city lights here. Maybe you noticed."

She caught the flashlight. "You're impossible."

"Makes you wonder why in hell we ever got married, doesn't it?"

She went still, riding the pain of that.

He swore under his breath. "I shouldn't have said that."

A lifetime of practice helped her lift her chin, her shoulder. "You're entitled to say anything you like, Sam. It's been no concern of mine what you say since we got *un*married."

The measuring look was back. And it was almost enough to make her uneasy. Almost. She clenched the flashlight and shoved her feet into her pumps, stifling a wince. That's what she got for indulging her shoe sense rather than her common sense when she'd dressed so very long ago before the flight. Then she snatched up her briefcase and strode past him, right on out the front door. As soon as it closed behind her, the dark night swallowed her whole, and she fumbled with the flashlight. It gave out a weak stream.

She stiffened her shoulders. Trained the wobbling

yellow beam in front of her. Headed up the stone walk. By the time she made it to the road that was only marginally smoother than the path, her feet were screaming inside her shoes. *She* wanted to scream. She was supposed to be an intelligent woman. Why hadn't she followed her common sense that giving Sam back the ring in person was a foolish idea? It wasn't as if he'd appreciate the sensitivity she'd been aiming for. She should have just taken the hint and kept the ring—tucked it away in some forgotten corner, in the same way she tucked away memories of *him*.

The only answer she got was a stone in the road that seemed to mock the notion of tucking Sam away anywhere as it caught her foot and sent her pitching forward.

She cried out. The flashlight flew out of her hand, her briefcase slid off her shoulder and her hands took the worst of the impact when she fell.

"You are the most stubborn woman God ever put on this earth."

Perfect. Her day was complete.

Her hands burned. Her bare heels burned. Her eyes burned, the contents of her briefcase were scattered about, and the flashlight had gone dead. It was, unfortunately, nowhere within hand's reach—she earned only another piece of gravel against her raw palms when she swept around feeling for it—or she could have used it to brain him.

She bowed her head. Violence never solved anything. "You were following me. I hope you got a good laugh." The way she felt, it could well be his last.

She heard him sigh. "There's usually more moonlight." He moved around in front of her, and she gasped when he crouched down and lifted her head. "You'd have been able to see better, even with that cheap flashlight."

"Obviously it's enough light for you," she said, jerking her chin away from his touch. "I hope you enjoyed the entertainment."

"Delaney—"

"What?"

He sighed again. "Shut up."

Her eyes burned anew when he caught her beneath her arms and helped her stand. She tested her footing. Frustration tightened her voice. "I think I broke my heel."

"What?" He swore and swept her up in his arms, heading back toward his house before she could blink.

She went board stiff. "Wait. My briefcase."

"Christ, Delaney, are you afraid you'll misplace some precious bit of work? I'll get it after I get you settled."

"But I don't—"

He kissed her again and shock swept through her, taking her words right along with it.

When he lifted his head, his breathing was rough. "At least there's still *one* way to get you to shut up."

She hastily closed her mouth, stemming her next words. *Put me down* screamed through her mind.

Sam grunted a little. "Better."

She shifted as far from him as humanly possible. Which wasn't far, given the fact that he had one arm around her back, his hand practically cupping the side of her breast. His other arm's position wasn't much better, tucked beneath her knees, causing her skirt to rumple up around her thighs. She surreptitiously tugged at the skirt. It didn't help. The more she moved, the less space she could keep between them. She settled for trying not to breathe as his long stride ate up the distance back to his house.

He carried her straight through, back to the kitchen again, settling her on a bar stool. "Sit tight. I'll get some ice."

Delaney looked at her palms. They were red, raw, dirty. "I need to wash first." She started to slide off the high bar stool.

"Dammit all, Delaney, would you just sit still?" He'd yanked open the freezer door.

"Don't bark at me." She focused on the bag of frozen peas he pulled from the freezer. "What…are you hungry now?"

"The bag's easier to use than ice."

It had always been hard to read his expressions, but just then Delaney thought he looked near the end of his patience.

Well, her patience was sorely limited, too. Particularly when he cupped her calf and lifted gently. He'd had his hands on her more in this one day than nearly the entire last month they'd been together.

"Which heel?"

She leaned over, pulling off her shoe, holding it up. "No amount of frozen peas is going to help it, I'm afraid."

He studied the shoe for a long moment. "I thought you meant your *heel.*"

"I realize that. Now. You, um, you can let go of my leg."

He did so. Quickly. She still felt the imprint of his gentle touch.

Distance. Distance was paramount.

She slid off the bar stool and scooted around him, awkwardly toeing off the other shoe at the same time. She hadn't thought to bring a spare pair. She sidled past him and carefully stuck her hands under the faucet.

"I'll get your briefcase."

How could she have managed to forget about it so quickly? "Right—" he'd pulled a very sturdy-looking flashlight from the same drawer that had held the other one. She swallowed the thanks she'd been about to voice. The flashlight he'd chosen for his own use undoubtedly had strong batteries. "Make sure you get everything," she said waspishly.

"Would you rather do it yourself?"

She shut off the water and snapped off a paper towel from the stone holder next to the sink. "It's your fault I fell in the first place. You could have just driven me back to Castillo House, and none of this would—"

"I thought assigning blame was against your professional ethics."

She looked at him, their past a sudden, deluging wave. "Janie mentioned that your father is here. Staying with… Etta…she said. How do you feel about that, Sam?"

His expression closed down, just as she'd known it would, just as it always had whenever she'd broached the subjects he'd deemed off-limits.

There'd been a time when she'd only wanted to

understand the man who'd finessed her heart right out from under her. So she'd probed. Delicately. Hopefully.

It made her ill that she now used the same knowledge about Sam to retaliate. Wound for wound.

"Sam, I'm sorry."

He never heard the words.

He'd already walked out of the room.

Chapter 3

Kissing her like that had been stupid.

Sam raked his hands through his hair. Pressed the heels of his palms against his eyes. Twenty-one months. He'd had to say that, hadn't he? As if he'd been counting.

He'd even picked up the contents of Delaney's briefcase after walking out of his own damn house. Papers. Pens. Cell phone. Organizer. A thin bag holding her personal items. When he'd finished, he'd contemplated pitching the entire thing off the cliff behind his house. Instead, he'd left the briefcase sitting on his front porch, and he'd driven back into town.

The bar fight he'd broken up earlier at the Seaspray couldn't have come at a more opportune time, as far as he was concerned. He'd almost tossed the two idiots in jail, just because it would've felt good to do so.

Instead, he'd sent them home and planted his own butt on the end stool—one of the few the Haggerty fools hadn't broken before he and Leo contained the fight. The Seaspray had once been a motel until a storm leveled it. So far, the only thing to be rebuilt was the bar. Mostly because the long wooden bar itself was the only thing that had been left standing.

He hunched over that bar, his hands cradling his mug. But he wasn't seeing the dark liquid. He was seeing Delaney's face; her expression when he'd kissed her. When he'd called her his wife.

In the opposite corner of the bar, his brother Leo slopped a cleaning rag over the bar stools.

"Sam?"

He looked up. And swore silently again. "Kind of late for you to be out, isn't it?"

It was a testament to Sara Drake's good nature that she didn't slap him when she slid onto the stool beside him. "Thought I'd check and see how you're doing. Went by the sheriff's office. Was heading home when I saw your SUV outside this place."

"You shouldn't have bothered."

"Maybe it's not a bother." Her smile flashed briefly. She nodded at Leo when he abandoned his cleaning rag to fill a glass with soda that he placed in front of her before he moved over to the small television at the far end of the bar.

Sam thought maybe he owed Sara an apology. But the Vega and Drake families went way back. Sam had grown up with Sara's brother, Logan. Long ago both he and Logan had left Turnabout Island.

They'd both returned.

And while he felt an apology was in order, he wasn't entirely certain why. Things weren't that way between him and Sara. They never had been. Never would be, even if he weren't still married and his kid brother wasn't hung up on her.

He picked up his mug and drained it before he spoke. "I should have told you."

"Why? There are things I haven't told you, either." Her smile widened a little. "Nothing quite as major as a marriage, mind you."

"You're too nice, Sara." He meant it. She was nice.

"Yeah," she agreed lightly. "All that niceness going to waste with no man around to take advantage of it."

Sam looked up to find her watching Leo as she spoke. "Don't expect your grandmother to be quite as understanding," she warned, sounding amused. Then she nudged his shoulder with hers, companionably, and sat forward, propping her elbow on the bar. "Funny that I never pictured you with the buttoned-down type," Sara murmured. "How'd you two meet?"

Buttoned-down type. Laney would detest that description. He'd have to remember it. "Working a case."

"And you don't want to talk about it."

"No."

"Well, that's fair enough." She was silent for a moment. "Janie told me she took Delaney to your place. Presumably you know that, by now."

He grunted noncommittally.

"Do we need to check your place for a body?"

His lips twitched. "Not yet."

"So, what are you doing here?"

He nudged his mug. "What's it look like?"

"Come on, Sam. You dropped the news that you're secretly married and walked out of Annie and Logan's party. And now, hours later, you're at a bar you detest. Did you leave her alone at your place or what?"

"Delaney's capable of fending for herself. Believe me." More than capable. The woman preferred it to ever depending on someone else. She could dredge up a wealth of trust for her patients, but had she had enough in him?

Had he deserved it? *No.*

Sara eyed him a moment longer. "Samson and Delaney. Kind of funny, isn't it? Almost like Samson and Delilah."

His wife had once been his only weakness. "Funny." Oh, yeah. Har-dee-har-har.

"Well." Sara slid off the bar stool. "I'm a good listener if you want to talk." Her tone was dry. They both knew Sam didn't share his thoughts with much of anybody. "Don't pour too much more of that stuff for the sheriff, here, Leo," she said as she headed toward the door. "It's lethal."

Sam barely waited for the door to close behind Sara. "Leo." He snagged his brother's attention from the television and lifted his empty mug.

Leo grimaced, then headed back over to Sam. "She's right, man, you're gonna be sorry."

"Pour."

Leo shook his head, regretfully. But he poured, then ambled back over to watch the remainder of his black-and-white midnight screamer.

Sam lifted the mug of what was hands-down the vilest coffee he'd ever tasted.

"Y'oughta have a beer," Leo said, not looking his way. "Or turpentine. Be easier on the stomach."

Easier didn't mean better. Given Sam's current frame of mind, once he started drinking he wasn't gonna want to stop until he couldn't remember that Delaney was still back at his place.

"You going to Etta's tomorrow?" Leo's voice interrupted his grim thoughts.

Sam twisted the coffee mug back and forth, lining it up with the permanent rings on the bar. "No."

"First time since you came back to the island that you're going to miss her Sunday dinner."

"She'll live." He wasn't in the mood to discuss his reasons for avoiding his grandmother's traditional Sunday meal. Leo knew the reasons well enough.

Leo shrugged. "Etta's gonna use your tail for dog chow if you don't show up tomorrow. With your wife in tow. Word travels fast around here. It's a wonder she hasn't already hunted you down about that particular bit."

Truth was, Sam was a little surprised at that, too. "I can handle Etta." And "towing" had never worked with Delaney.

Leo's lips quirked. He looked back at the television. Then the clock. The bar would close at two. Not a minute before, not a minute later, whether there were patrons present or not.

"Heard she's good-looking."

"Etta? That's where you get the looks, Leo," Sam deadpanned.

His brother shot him the bird. Some described Henrietta Vega as a handsome woman. Sam considered her a tough old bird. In looks as well as personality. He loved her, but generally—aside from her fried chicken and mashed potatoes—she was a source of regular irritation.

"Did you leave her or was it the other way around?"

No respite. No need to clarify who Leo was speaking of. "Depends who you ask," he said truthfully, and stood. "Don't let the Haggerty boys back in here for a few days. Vern's been aching for trouble since he got booted from the academy."

"Their money's good."

"Their brains aren't. Those two are spoiling for a fight about something and getting drunk isn't helping. Next time they might do more damage than bust up a few bar stools."

Leo nodded. "Yeah, whatever. Go home to your wife and stop lecturing me." There was no heat in Leo's voice.

Sam left.

Go home to your wife. Now there was a damned strange thing to consider.

Too strange to do just yet. Instead, he drove up and down Turnabout Road. Going slowly, looking over the sleeping town. Sara's moonlit fields where she and Annie grew crops for their shop of lotions and herbal goops. Diego Montoya's recently rebuilt dock where his ancient ferry rocked in the water, making soft thumps and gentle rattles. Then back up to the road to the far end of the isle where the gates of Castillo House were closed. A few windows in the big house glowed yellow in the night, but the Christmas lights from the party were all dark.

His tires crunched over gravel and crumbling blacktop as he turned the vehicle around. Eight-point-seven miles straight down the only real road the island possessed and he was back at his own place.

No glowing windows welcomed him home.

He turned off the engine, leaving the key in the ignition. Nobody on the island would steal his truck. There would be no place to go with it.

He went inside, heading straight to his room. It wasn't his imagination that caught Delaney's scent as he walked through the dark house. It was the same custom perfume that she'd liked before.

He shook off the memory and moved to the glass door that opened onto the rear deck. But his hand paused as he glanced out.

She'd turned on the outdoor light and though it wasn't very bright, he could plainly see Delaney sitting in one of the chairs on the narrow deck. That surprised him. Though she had pushed the chair as close to the house as it would go to put more distance between her and the rail overlooking the cliff. What didn't surprise him was the file that she was reading, occasionally scrawling some note.

He stood there, silently, watching her for a long while, knowing she wouldn't be able to see him standing there in the dark even if she did look his way. She was as slender as ever, her crossed legs as long and shapely as his dreams frequently reminded. Tailored, no frills and completely female with a love for shoes that made her ankles look even finer. He'd always been torn between male appreciation of her unabashedly sexy shoes and amusement that the things were hazardous. His gaze drifted down to her bare feet. Her toenails were painted red and that was new. Not at all the subtle pastel stuff she'd worn before. She'd also taken down her hair. The white-blond gleam of it drifted around her slender shoulders. From the day he'd met her, she'd confined her hair. In pins, or a ponytail. He still remembered the feel of the silky strands the first time he'd pulled the hair free. He closed his fingers against the itch in his palms.

Now, either she was playing some game that completely escaped him, or she really did believe they were divorced.

Both seemed implausible ideas when it came to Delaney.

He abruptly slid open the door and her head whipped around at the sound. "You can use the guest room," he said before she could speak. "The bed's not made. I'll have to find you some sheets."

She closed the file in her briefcase and pushed out of the padded chair to face him. The breeze lifted her hair. "I already did. Make the bed, that is."

"Efficient of you."

"Don't look at me like that. It was something to do since I've been stuck here for the past few hours."

He stepped closer to her, getting in her space. He'd learned a long time ago that it was one of the only ways to break through that mile-high reserve of hers. Most people would simply step away from someone invading their personal space, but not Delaney. Not when she had an even higher share of pride than reserve.

And underneath it all a boundless heart that occasionally snuck out and showed through her soft blue eyes. "I'm surprised you came out on the deck," he murmured. "It's pretty high up from the water."

"Actually, it's rather like being surrounded by the sky," she said coolly.

Of course. Commenting on her fear of heights put that extra tone in her voice. "You have circles under your eyes."

"Flattery always was your strong point, Sam."

"You still don't get enough sleep. Probably too busy reading case files in bed."

She pressed her palm to her throat, her eyes going wide. "And here, all this time I thought you didn't care."

"Nice to know we still bring out the best in each other."

She didn't bat an eye. "Isn't it? And I'll *take* your kind offer of the guest room with my assurance that I'll leave as soon as humanly possible. I'll catch Mr. Montoya's ferry first thing."

"You can cut the act, Delaney. There's nobody here but us."

"Act." Her brows drew together. "Were you always so...unpleasant?"

He almost laughed at that. "There were times you didn't think so." He touched the ends of her silky hair, a genuine smile tugging at his lips when her bravado disappeared in a puff. Something about her eyes. One moment they frothed like a whitecap and the next they were quiet pools that hid none of the depths inside her.

She shifted, adding a good foot of distance between them. "Really? I hardly remember."

He had to give her credit for trying.

He turned back toward his room. "Come through here. Guest room's across the hall, but you probably figured that out when you were hunting up sheets in my closets."

She hurriedly snatched up the briefcase, following him. "I didn't snoop."

"Did I accuse you of it?"

"You implied it."

He exhaled noisily. "Get some sleep, Delaney. And forget about catching Diego's ferry tomorrow."

"Why on earth would I want to do that?"

He knew if he looked at her, the whitecaps would be back. He knew if he looked at her, he'd want to touch her again, no matter how stupid it would be. "It doesn't run on Sundays."

She was silent a moment. "Dandy."

Delaney was the only person he'd ever known who used the word *dandy,* much less for circumstances ranging from spectacular to abysmal. He sat on the end of his bed and then—because he was a man and she was his wife—he couldn't help but look at her. "Not exactly like running to the corner and hailing a cab."

"No."

He pulled off one boot. Go away, Laney.

Her eyebrows drew together. "Are you trying to intimidate me?"

"By taking off my boots?" He removed the other and it hit the floor with a thud to lie by the first. "I'm not that obvious." Yes, he was. Go away, Laney.

"By making me uncomfortable, you can control the situation."

He stood and started on his shirt buttons. "Like this?"

"You're so obvious."

"And you're not moving." He tossed the shirt aside. "Maybe because you want to stay. The bedroom really was where we did all our best work."

"Bedroom?" The word burst from her lips. "Half the time you—"

"I…what?" He prompted when her voice strangled down to nothing. "Didn't wait to get to the bedroom?" He took a step toward her. And another. For each step he took, she inched farther away, the briefcase held in front of her like a shield. The door was within reach.

"Remember that time we—"

The phone rang.

She jumped a little.

He considered ignoring it. But he couldn't. He was the bloody sheriff; the only law in a town that had a council but no mayor, because nobody wanted to take on the job of heading up the antiquated place. He eyed Delaney as it rang again.

She looked pale.

He was surprised she didn't use the phone as her last means of escape. But then there were lots of things he'd found surprising about Delaney.

He went over to the bed and snatched up the extension. "Vega." The airy hum over the line meant the call wasn't local. Not the Haggerty boys getting into it again, then. "Hello?"

"Detective Vega?"

It'd been a while since he'd been called that. "Not anymore. Who is this?" But he knew the answer before the other man answered.

"Chad Wright."

"Yeah?" Sam's voice was bland.

The line hummed for a moment. Then Chad cleared his throat. "Well, I was looking for my fiancée."

Fiancée.

Well, well, well.

Sam shoved his hand in his pocket to keep from tearing the phone out of the wall and slid his gaze to Delaney. "Who would that be," he asked genially, knowing full well that it was the woman standing in the doorway of his bedroom, eyeing him suspiciously.

"Delaney, of course." Chad sounded impatient. "Look, I know it's late. But she never checked into the hotel in San Diego, and I haven't been able to reach her on her cell phone. She said she planned to speak with you after she'd taken care of some business there, and I'm just trying to locate her. I've already checked with Castillo House, and she left there hours ago. Do you know if she was delayed in Turnabout?"

On Turnabout. It's an island. Idiot. But not such an idiot that his concern kept him from calling Sam—something the other man had to have hated doing. "Cell phones don't work out here."

"Yes, I figured that out. So? Have you seen her?"

He held the phone in Delaney's direction. "Your fiancé's on the phone for you."

Her ivory skin went white. She pushed back her hair from her face. "Chad?"

"You engaged to more than one guy?"

She didn't answer that. The fine line of her jaw tightened. She set her case down on the dresser by the door before quickly moving forward to snatch the phone. She turned her back on him, but she couldn't go far. It was a corded phone, as good as a leash.

Her voice was low, but Sam could still hear her as she greeted Chad Wright. Chadly Do-Wright.

And his wife was engaged to him.

He moved to the foot of the bed and sat down. He'd be damned if he'd leave, but listening to the muted one-sided conversation took him perilously close to the end of his rope.

The divorce proceedings she'd once started had long ago been dismissed, incomplete. She could well have filed again. Technically, he *had* abandoned her. Moved out of their apartment. Her apartment, to be precise.

Hell, he'd moved out of the state, to the opposite side of the country. Wasn't surprising that Chad had made a move on her.

Was surprising that Delaney had accepted. She'd always claimed there was nothing romantic between them.

When she hung up, he still didn't move. He looked at the palms of his hands, entertaining the vision of slamming them into Do-Wright's perfectly tanned blondness. "So that's what this is about. Return one ring. Exchange it for another." He looked up at her, keeping his hands from fisting through sheer willpower. "Are you actually going to *wear* it this time?"

Her eyes shimmered. "Sam—"

"Come on, honey. Don't be tongue-tied now."

"Don't call me honey."

"I suppose the endearment's reserved for the good Dr. Wright now."

"I'm not discussing Chad with you."

"Why not? I think a husband should be able to discuss his wife's lover, don't you?"

Whitecaps frothed, then iced over. She looked incensed. "Chad is not my lover. And even if he were, it'd be no business of yours, because I am not your wife anymore!" Her voice rose.

Maybe in a few years he'd look back and find some humor in this. Like when he was dead in the ground about a hundred years.

He pushed to his feet and closed his hands over her shoulders, feeling her jump, before backing her to the doorway of his bedroom until she stood in the hall. He took his hands away from her and handed her the briefcase.

His wife.

The only woman he'd ever loved, and the only woman whose lack of trust in him had nearly killed him.

"Yes," he said almost gently. "You are."

Then he closed the door in her face.

Chapter 4

Delaney stared at the door for only a moment before she dumped her briefcase on the floor and reached for the handle.

But something inside her paused.

Could it be?

Her fingers curled against her palm.

No. Couldn't be, she assured herself firmly and reached for the handle and turned it. She pushed the door inward, but couldn't make herself take a step into the bedroom to save her soul.

Sam was sitting again on the foot of the bed. Hunched forward, muscles clearly defined under a satin layer of bronze skin. His arms were braced on his thighs, hands loose, relaxed, between. She met his unreadable dark eyes.

"I don't believe you," she said baldly. As if the words could make it so.

He merely quirked an eyebrow. "There's a surprise."

"What do you hope to gain by this pretense? It's so easily disproved."

"Then go ahead and do that, Delaney. Disprove it. You'll need to before you pledge your troth to Do-Wright."

"Leave Chad out of this."

"Why? Seems he's officially part of the threesome now." His voice was mocking. "Like it or not, Delaney, you are—" his jaw tightened "—my wife."

"I've got the papers that say otherwise!"

"Really. Well, I've got the papers that say the action was dismissed because of incomplete paperwork."

"I had an attorney, Sam. He wouldn't have made a mistake like that."

He rose and it was like watching something dangerous uncoil. "Hope you don't depend on him too often, then." He slid open a drawer in his bureau and pulled out a thick manila envelope. "Read it and weep, darlin'." He held it out to her.

She didn't believe him. He was playing some sort of game for reasons known only to him.

Yet she found herself walking into his bedroom—not a smart place to be in the best of circumstances—to take the envelope.

"Takes only one paper to get married, but takes a stack two inches thick to get unmarried."

She ignored his black comment as she unfastened the metal tab holding the envelope closed and slid out the contents. The same contents that were in the same size envelope her attorney had mailed her a year ago.

Only, you were such a basket case, you put the envelope in the closet without ever looking at it.

She rested the papers on Sam's bureau. Her chest ached from the hard beat of her heart and she had to stare hard, read twice, to make sense of the cover letter.

And when she did, the bottom of her stomach seemed to drop out.

The judge had dismissed the petition because the filing had not been properly completed.

"Dismissed on a technicality," Sam murmured behind her. "Seen it happen time and again in criminal cases."

Delaney thrust back her hair and read the letter again. But of course the contents hadn't magically changed just because she was on the verge of losing it.

"Why didn't you say something?"

"When? During our weekly telephone chats?"

Her lips tightened. Until that evening she hadn't spoken with Sam since the day he'd moved out of their apartment. "You could have called."

"You're the one who filed, Delaney," he reminded, and his even, reasonable tone set her teeth on edge. "Not me. When the time period the judge gave to correct the omissions passed and nothing happened, I figured that was your decision, too. Hope you didn't pay your lawyer too much, though. Not that you'd miss it, with the Townsend family bank account at your disposal, but—"

"Stop it." She whirled around to face him, managing to scatter the papers across the smooth wood surface. If she *had* used the Townsend attorney, none of this would be happening now. But she'd been determined to keep the matter in her control, and look at the results.

"Suppose you want to call Do-Wright."

She started. Chad. The furthest person from her mind. "We're still married."

"Yeah."

"We're still married."

"Are you shooting for the say-it-three-times-and-click-your-heels thing? It's not going to change things, and there's no Good Witch on Turnabout who can wave a magic wand."

"How nice you find this amusing, Sam. What if I'd—"

"Already walked the white carpet with Do-Wright?" The corner of his lip lifted. "Would have put an interesting title behind your name. Might have caused some curiosity with your colleagues. Bigamy—"

"Stop!" She launched herself at him, pushing at his chest. Some part of her sane self watched on in horror. "Can't you take anything seriously for once?"

He'd barely swayed from her attack. "I take plenty of things seriously," he assured. "Just not you marrying Chad Wright. What the hell were you thinking, Delaney? He gives *bland* new meaning. He'll bore you to tears."

"He's not boring, he's calm."

"He's a wimp and you'll walk all over him."

"We're in perfect accord with our plans."

"Which include what? Working side by side seventy hours of the week? Hell, baby, you already did that without being married to him."

She mentally dragged herself back from being drawn further into a verbal battle. "There's no point in rehashing the past."

"Particularly when there was never any initial hashing."

"We communicated," she defended.

"We argued and we made love. Two things we did supremely well." His gaze dropped to her lips. "Can you say the same about Do-Wright?"

She felt the flush rise in her cheeks and damned the fact that it had more to do with the way he looked at her than anything else. "I've already said that Chad and I aren't lovers. I refuse to let you beat me over the head with that."

"Engaged, *thinking* you were free to marry, and you two never slept together?" His eyebrow rose. "You've been colleagues since before you and I even met four years ago, and you've never..." He shook his head. "Doesn't that make you wonder, just a little, Delaney? I mean the guy does like women, doesn't he? He's milquetoast compared to you. How do you think he'll react when he finds out that under your sleek, refined exterior, you're a firecracker in bed?"

She slapped him. Then stared at the outline of her hand on his cheek with shock.

The corner of his lip kicked up. "And you always preach that violence is never the answer."

"You're despicable."

"Maybe. But I'm right, and you know it."

"What does it matter to you, anyway, Sam? It's not as if you *want* to be married to me. You left, remember?

Walked out, taking hardly anything but the clothes on your back with you. And you didn't just leave me. You left your job. You left the state, for God's sake. I only found out that you'd come here because my father checked the precinct for me to see what forwarding address you'd left!"

And hadn't *that* been a humiliating experience? Her father had made no secret that he blamed her for Sam's departure. But then, her dad was good at blaming her. She'd known perfectly well that he preferred Sam's company to her own.

"Missed me, did you?"

"I'm going to bed," she said flatly. "Alone," she added before he could make some comment. "And tomorrow I'll get off this island even if I have to swim to do it." She turned on her heel and strode from the room, slamming the door behind her.

He was impossible. He'd always been impossible. She made her living working with people. She believed that nobody was a lost cause, that the mind and the emotions of a person were never beyond hope.

But Sam was…Sam.

And being a psychiatrist hadn't gotten her any closer to understanding him than it had to understanding herself.

"Impossible," she muttered, grabbing her briefcase again and hurrying into the guest room, closing—and locking—that door. Just in case.

She wished she could lock the door on her memories just as easily, but they pushed in on her relentlessly.

* * *

"What are you doing here?" Catcher Dan's was her dad's favorite tavern. Though the department had given him a formal retirement dinner, it was here that the boys and girls in blue were giving Captain Randall Townsend his true sendoff. Whether her dad expected it or not, Delaney felt she should be there. What she hadn't expected was to see Detective Vega there, as well.

He wasn't wearing a suit, for once. The dozen times she'd seen him since he'd first come to her office seeking information about a patient of hers he'd been in a suit and tie, albeit a loosened tie.

Now he wore blue jeans that fit obscenely well and a Hawaiian print shirt. Untucked.

He had his index finger wrapped around a sweating longneck beer. He tilted the bottle in greeting. It was marginally more polite than her greeting had been.

"Everybody wants to send off the captain," he said, leaning toward her so she could hear him over the din.

Delaney sat back as far as the mahogany bar behind her would allow. It was one thing to square off with the man across her desk or a judge's chambers. Another entirely to be cramped together in a bar that ought to be closed down for exceeding the maximum occupancy. "You've never come to his parties before." Not Randall's birthday celebration. Not the departmental holiday celebrations.

Sam's lips tilted. He leaned forward again. Just a few inches. Just enough to make her blood rush a little faster.

"Didn't know you were missing me," he said. He reached past her, setting his beer on the bar. He left his hand propped on the curved wood.

Delaney felt surrounded by him.

It wasn't altogether unpleasant. The whiff of his aftershave was rather like getting a first breath of ocean wind. Faintly spicy. Decidedly fresh. She buried her nose in her wineglass, acknowledging his comment with a noncommittal nod.

His head dipped close to hers again. "When are you going to have dinner with me?"

He hadn't asked her that since the first day they'd met two years ago. She'd refused. Had considered him judgmental and unfeeling. And had definitely held his profession against him. He was a cop. She didn't need more cops in her life. "I don't date."

"Wasn't asking for a date. Just dinner."

She smiled, despite herself. "The difference being?"

"Professional."

Her smile died. "If you're seeking a therapist, go through the department. If you're talking about my sessions with Alonso Petrofski—" She realized his eyes were smiling. "Oh. You're—"

"Joking. Yeah. We've battled enough over Petrofski in the past two years. This is supposed to be a retirement celebration. You don't look very celebratory."

"Don't be ridiculous." She smiled even more cheerfully and lifted her glass. "Celebrating away."

His lashes were thick. Spiky. Longer than her own. He really was attractive in a dark, intense way. She felt the warmth of his gaze on her face and lifted her glass again, draining it far too quickly.

"Why don't you?"

Her head felt a little muzzy. Cigar smoke, loud laughter, louder music, and too hastily drunk wine. She hardly even realized that it was she who leaned closer to him to be heard. "Why don't I what?"

"Date."

She turned her head to look up at him, only to find his face mere inches from hers. She swallowed. Her heart thumped a crazy little beat. Lord. A tilt of her chin and she could press her lips to his.

In the far reaches of her mind, she heard a burst of applause. As if the universe were cosmically urging her to do just that.

Then she realized the cheering was for the retiring Captain Townsend. Her face felt hot as she leaned back again. There hadn't really been such a small distance between her and Sam, she assured herself.

She focused her attention on her father, who was standing front and center on the tiny dais in the corner of the bar. He was tall, his blond hair graying into elegant silver. He held a mug of beer in one hand and a cigar in the other and he was grinning, even though Delaney knew the last thing in the world her father wanted to do was retire from the force.

He waved down the cheers and chatter.

Sam drew his finger along Delaney's arm.

She swallowed and focused harder on her father's hale-and-hearty speech. She knew the drill. She was the captain's daughter; his only remaining family since the death of her brother more than a decade earlier. Any minute now he'd throw out his arm and invite her up there with him. And she'd tilt her glass to him, give him a kiss and share a joke—God knew what—about how great it would be having him around more.

Sam's finger drifted over her wrist.

She drew in a much-needed breath and slid off the bar stool. Looked at him, listening to her father with half an ear.

There was something uncommonly still about Sam, she decided. And yet something excruciatingly alive in his gaze.

Then her father's words penetrated. "…all of us raise a toast to the one person I wish could have been here tonight. My son, Randy."

More cheers. More drinking. Captain Randall Townsend stepped off the dais and was immediately surrounded by his backslapping well-wishers.

Delaney stood there. Her eyes prickled. Her throat burned. The wine she'd consumed rose.

Sam wrapped his arm around her waist and somehow she found herself standing outside, gulping in great gasps of chilly night air.

"Here." Sam pushed a glass—she didn't know from where—into her hand. "Drink."

The sidewalk seemed to undulate beneath her feet. "I've had enough to drink. More than enough."

"It's water."

She drank. When the squat glass was empty, she cradled it in her palm, staring down.

"Better?"

"Yes." No. But at least she didn't feel in danger of losing her lunch anymore.

"What was that all about in there?"

She stared harder into the empty glass. Maybe if she stared hard enough, the tears burning behind her eyes wouldn't fall. "My father's retiring," she stated the obvious.

He took the glass from her and set it on the stoop. There was a collection of other glasses already there. Before the bar closed, they'd be cleared away. Then he folded her hands in his. "A fact that causes you tears?"

Simple human contact. It was definitely underrated. What else could stir the words to her mouth? "There are two things my father has loved," she said huskily. "His son and his career. Now he's losing the second thing, as well."

Sam's thumbs moved over the backs of her hands. Warmth seeped into her cold fingers. "I'd heard the captain lost a son a long time ago. What happened?"

Cold again. "You want the official version, or my father's?"

"Yours."

"It was an automobile accident. The car went off an embankment." She looked up at him. Felt the intensity of his dark brown gaze right through to her bones.

Even though she knew she could stop with just that much information, she continued, "He died. I didn't." The words were bald, but they held the bottom line.

She couldn't bring herself to admit she'd been arguing with Randy, begging him to pull over so she could drive. That she'd tracked him down at a fraternity party, dragged him out minutes before the party was raided by cops from her dad's own precinct. If she'd left alone, he'd have been arrested like his frat brothers instead of behind the wheel of his car that she'd jumped into, still trying to "save" him from himself.

If she'd left him alone, the accident would never have happened.

After a moment Sam exhaled. He let go of her hands only to tuck her hand through the crook of his arm. It was a courtly gesture. "Come on."

She realized she'd walked half a block with him before it occurred to her to ask where they were going.

"My place."

She absorbed that. Felt acutely aware that he waited for her to tell him no. Just as acutely aware that he wasn't pressing or persuading. That he would accept her answer, either way.

That he was the only one in an entire room of her dad's cronies—people she'd had surrounding her nearly all of her life—who'd noticed that she was at all affected by her father's speech.

She curled her fingers more closely against the curve of Sam's bicep. Her heart skittered around inside her chest.

And they continued walking.

The door vibrated at her back, and the past slid back into the past. Delaney blinked, staring across at the bed that she'd made with sheets she'd found in a hall linen closet. They'd been neatly folded. Smelling fresh. She'd been unable to stop her speculation of who'd done Sam's laundry because he'd never been known to do it before. Then she'd sat out on the deck, waiting for him to reappear, wondering if he would reappear.

The door vibrated again. She turned and yanked it open after fumbling with the lock, too many emotions to decipher tangling inside her. "What?" She glared up at Sam. Sam, four years older than when they'd first met, barely two years older than that night outside Catcher Dan's when their relationship took a fateful turn. But he was no less disturbing. With or without his shirt. And he still smelled faintly of a wild ocean breeze.

"I asked if you needed toothpaste."

What she needed was her own head examined. "What?"

"Toothpaste. To go with that little toothbrush with its own case that you still carry around."

Her face heated. "What are we doing now, Sam? Having a perfectly inconsequential exchange over my toiletries?"

"Do you need some damn toothpaste or not?"

"No." The little case also had room for its own tiny tube. "Ever tidy."

"Prepared." Only that wasn't really true. If she'd been prepared, she'd never have gotten into this situation in the first place. "Is that it? Or do you have some other bombshell you'd like to drop on me just for kicks."

His eyes narrowed. "No."

Her stomach tightened. The bed behind her loomed large in her mind, even though she knew better than to think Sam would ever use force. He'd never needed to.

"Here." He shoved a bundle into her arms. "So you don't get cold." Then he turned and crossed the hall, disappearing into his own room. The door closed with a soft click.

She looked down at the items. Thick white socks. A large, faded blue sweatshirt with the collar cut out.

Her cold bare toes curled.

She eyed the panel of his bedroom door for a long while.

Still married.

The reality of it plunged over her and with a shaking hand, she closed her door again and stumbled to the bed, clutching the sweatshirt and socks like some sort of life preserver that had no hope of saving her.

Chapter 5

The voices Delaney heard coming from the kitchen the next morning nearly sent her back to the quasi sanctuary of the guest bedroom. To hide out. To indulge her own cowardice.

She smoothed back her hair. Her narrow black slacks and white tunic were made for traveling and were presentable, but her feet were bare thanks to the broken heel on her shoe. Hardly the optimum conditions in which to face Sam and his morning visitors.

It was her own stupidity, of course, that led to this. She should have been better prepared for Sam.

As if anyone could ever be prepared for *him*.

She entered the kitchen, stopping just inside the entryway. Sam stood at the stove, his back to her.

He was cooking.

A newly acquired skill, or just one he'd never exercised when they'd been married?

You are still married.

She mentally told the voice in her head to put a sock in it and thanked her stars that none of her patients could see her now. She'd lose all credibility.

Janie sat at the granite countertop alongside a young girl with a mop of blond curls who was watching Sam's actions at the stove with evident glee. "Come on, Sam," Janie was saying. "You can't disappoint Etta any more than you could disappoint April wanting your French toast."

"Not now, Janie." Sam turned to the counter, sliding a plate in front of the little girl. Then he looked over his shoulder, clearly unsurprised to see her standing there. "Want coffee?"

"Yes." Mindful of his visitors, she made herself walk forward and add a thank-you.

He flipped a mug off a hook and filled it, then handed it to her. They could have been strangers, as if the previous day had never occurred.

She lifted the mug and rounded the countertop, aiming for the third of the four bar stools. The coffee was good. No surprise. Sam's coffee had always been better than hers. It was the only thing he'd ever done in the kitchen.

Besides you.

Shut up, voice.

She slid onto the stool and smiled at the little girl who

was watching her curiously. "I'm Delaney," she finally said when it seemed apparent nobody was taking charge of introductions.

"I'm April. My grandma is Maisy Fielding." Vivid green eyes behind thick glasses stared up at her.

"She has the inn I've heard about."

April nodded, then forked a bite of French toast and sliced banana into her little bow mouth. She'd barely swallowed before she spoke. "She lets me come with Janie every weekend for Sheriff Sam's French toast. Are you going to live here now with him?"

Delaney nearly choked on her sip of coffee. She carefully set down the mug. She didn't dare look at Sam. "I have a home, actually. In New York."

April continued watching her for a moment. Her gaze seemed peculiarly intense. Then she looked back at her plate without comment and continued eating.

"Here." Sam pushed a plate in front of her. French toast. No bananas. He'd remembered she was allergic to them.

Still, there was enough to feed a lumberjack. "The coffee's plenty," she protested.

"Eat." His voice was flat.

"Good grief, Sam," Janie chided. "Single-syllable commands are for dogs."

"You're too skinny, so eat." Sam's eyebrow rose. "Better?"

Delaney knew her face was flushed when Janie and April looked her way. "Such a way with words," she murmured.

April giggled. Janie rolled her eyes. Sam ignored her.

Once her coffee reached half-mast, she picked up her fork to defend against the hollow rumbling in her stomach. Certainly not because of Sam's order. She'd never been good at following orders. Not her father's. Not Sam's. The only one in her life smart enough not to try was Chad.

And *he'd* told Sam that they were engaged.

She set down her fork. "I need to get a new pair of shoes." And to get off the island.

"The store's closed on Sundays," April said. She was pushing a last bedraggled slice of banana around her plate, soaking up every drop of maple syrup.

Great. "Does someone other than Mr. Montoya have a boat that could take me across?"

"No."

Her mouth closed. She eyed Sam. He was loading the dishwasher. The picture of domesticity. Except for the badge on his leather belt and the unwelcoming glint in his dark eyes.

"Turnabout's a little old-fashioned that way," Janie provided. She carried her plate to the sink and rinsed it before handing it to Sam. Delaney felt the speculation in the young woman's eyes as she looked from Sam back to her again. "Diego's livelihood is the ferry. Nobody encroaches on that."

"What if there's an emergency?"

Sam spoke. "Replacing your broken-heeled shoe isn't one."

She felt her jaw tighten. "I wasn't suggesting that it was."

His lips twisted. He knew why she was anxious to leave.

Janie had rounded the counter again. "We're about the same size. I'm sure we can find something to work for you until tomorrow."

"Her feet are as skinny as the rest of her. I'll drive her into town," Sam countered abruptly. "Get Sophie Sheffield to open the store. See if she's got anything narrow enough."

"*The* store. As in there's only one?"

"Carries everything from apples to zippers." Sam looked at her. "Maybe not imported Italian shoes, but we make do."

If he was waiting for a derogatory comment, he'd wait a long while. And even though she realized going with Janie probably meant going to his grandmother's house—more family—she was less disturbed by that idea than by remaining with Sam. "Thanks for the offer of a loan, Janie. I'll take you up on it, if you don't mind." She cast Sam a small smile.

"Janie," he said, his expression not changing one whit, "don't you need to get April back to her grandmother's?"

Janie's dark gaze bounced from her brother to Delaney. She looked distinctly uncomfortable.

Delaney pushed her fingers inside her pockets rather than wring Sam's neck. "Maybe later," she suggested.

Janie started to nod.

"There won't be any need later," he countered flatly. "Sophie will open the store for me."

Delaney's jaw ached. "Fine."

"Well, okay then." Janie's voice was deliberately cheerful. "April, let's get going."

April slid off the bar stool. Only then did Delaney realize how badly the girl's vision was impaired. She moved comfortably, as if she were familiar with the layout of Sam's house. But there was no mistaking the way she counted steps, brushed her knuckles against objects, keeping her bearing.

Blind. Or nearly so.

"It was nice meeting you, Mrs. Sam." April held out her hand, clearly waiting for Delaney to take it.

She did, her heart squeezing a little. The child's expression was cheerful. "Call me Delaney," she said.

April's fingers tightened around hers for a second. "I like Mrs. Sam better." Then she gave a sunny smile and left with Janie.

"I hope you're satisfied," Delaney said the moment they heard the soft thump of the front door shutting. "Your sister was embarrassed."

"She's a big girl. I think she can handle it."

"You want to keep me away from your family, don't you? You never told them we were married in the first place, and you still don't want me having anything to do with them. What are you afraid of? That I'll contaminate the Vega family with the Townsend germs?"

"Do you want a fresh pair of socks? You might as well have something on your feet when we go to see Sophie and I doubt you want me to cut off the heel of your other shoe to match the broken one."

So much for communicating. "I'll go barefoot," she

said tightly. Better that than to put on something that belonged to him. It was bad enough that she'd slipped into his socks and sweatshirt sometime around dawn.

After which she'd finally found a brief measure of peaceful sleep.

"Fine." He headed from the kitchen. "I'm not bringing the shoes to you, Delaney."

She made a face at his back and hurried after him. If he didn't want to give her time to get her wallet, then he could just pay for what she needed himself. It was his fault her heel had broken in the first place, after all.

The stone walk was rough under her feet and she was glad to climb into his SUV even if it did mean being confined in a small space with him.

She kept as close to the door as possible without being obvious about it, but figured by the sidelong look he gave her that he knew what she was doing. Fortunately, the drive to town took only minutes. He pulled in front of a smallish cottage in a row of them and got out. "Wait here."

She mentally snapped a salute, but kept her comments to herself. She watched him stride up the narrow, short walk to the front door. It was opened almost immediately, and a round woman stepped out on the porch. Not two seconds passed before she was looking around Sam toward the vehicle.

Delaney pushed her lips into a smile. If she wasn't mistaken, she saw curtains twitching in the windows all down the row of cottages.

She suddenly felt like a fish in a fishbowl.

Sam was heading back to the SUV. He opened the passenger door. "Move over."

She slid to the center of the bench seat as he helped Sophie up inside, then rounded the truck to get behind the wheel.

"I appreciate this," Delaney told the woman after Sam's short introduction.

Sophie just nodded, her bright eyes studying Delaney as if she were some foreign object.

With the other woman's considerable self, the confined space in the front seat was even more so. What she *should* have done was climb into the rear seat rather than obey Sam's command. Thank heavens the island was as small as it was. From her shoulder to her knee, she felt every move Sam made as he turned the truck on the bumpy, narrow road and drove down the main road of the island to the end of the shops and buildings where Sophie's place was located.

It was marked ingeniously. The sign said The Store.

Sam helped Sophie from the truck and as the woman went to unlock, he looked at Delaney. "I don't need assistance getting out of this truck," she assured for his ears only. "So keep your hands to yourself."

The corner of his mouth kicked up. "Your desperation is showing, Delaney."

She slid to the ground. The sidewalk was cracked and rough, but she sailed past him, anyway, and entered the store behind Sophie.

"Shoes are in the back," the woman said, her voice huffing a little. "Clothes, too."

Delaney nodded and headed down the closest narrow aisle. It was jammed with toiletries. The store was larger than it appeared from the outside. After the jam-packed aisles in the front, it widened toward the rear. Hardware and tools on one side. Clothing in the center. Sporting goods on the other side.

She headed past an enormous fishing net to the rack of shoes. There wasn't a large selection, but she settled on a pair of rubber flip-flops in a virulent shade of pink. No fashion awards, but they stayed on her feet, at least.

She wore them to the front where Sophie and Sam waited.

"New look for you," he said blandly. "You need anything else? No?" He pulled out his wallet and handed Sophie a few bills then headed for the door. Sophie stayed put on her stool behind the cash register.

"You're not taking Sophie home?"

Sophie waved her hand. "Now that I'm here, I'll stay and work awhile. You two go on now. You don't need a third wheel." She smiled a little, as if she knew just how two married people who've been apart a long while would prefer to spend their Sunday.

Dandy. "Well. Thank you, again."

Sam was waiting at the door. As she went through, he dropped his arm over her shoulder. Delaney caught a glimpse of Sophie's satisfied expression as the door closed behind them.

She shrugged off his arm. "What are you doing?"

"Making Sophie's day." He rounded the truck. "She'll forgive me for not dating her daughter now that she knows I've got such a loving wife even if she *is* from off-island."

"Oh, very funny." She climbed up on the seat and tugged at the slipping neckline of her shirt. For all she knew, Sam had been treated to a constant parade of eligible women since he'd returned to Turnabout. Lord knew his looks were appealing enough. "Considering the way you were dancing with Sara Drake last night, I'd have thought you wouldn't need to provide any reason other than her."

"Jealous?"

"Hardly."

He shook his head slightly then drove a short distance before parking again, this time in front of a modest brick building. The sheriff's office.

"Duty calls even on a Sunday?"

He hung his wrist over the steering wheel and eyed her. "Do you really want to know how many hours I put in on the job?"

She'd stepped right into that one. No one to blame but herself. "No."

His lips tightened. "Didn't think so."

Annoyance rippled through her, but it was the guilt and grief that never fully left her that overcame her reserve. "I had patients who needed me, Sam."

Sam pushed open his door and stepped out. He wasn't up for that particular trip down memory lane. "You can come in or wait. Up to you."

"How long is the wait going to be?"

As long as he could make it. He shrugged.

Her soft lips compressed. "I need to use a phone."

"Worried about what Do-Wright's going to think when you tell him the news? You can use the station's phone."

"With you standing by listening in? I don't think so."

"Walk down to the community center, then." He pointed. "The big building over there. There's a pay phone." Which *didn't* work just as often as it did.

"I don't have my calling card with me. Someone rushed me out without giving me a chance to get my wallet."

"Life stinks, doesn't it?"

He closed the door and headed around the truck to unlock the station. The blinds covering the window on the top half of the door swayed when he went inside. He flipped on a light, dispelling the gloom of the cloudy morning and went over to his desk. The fact was, unless the Haggerty boys got rowdy or something unusual happened, there was little for him to do.

But, on the off chance that Delaney did come inside, he flipped open a folder of items that needed to be filed and set to it.

It wasn't long before his door rattled, the blinds swayed, and Delaney stood there. "The phone doesn't work." Her expression implied that it was somehow his fault.

"I'll put in a repair order," he said. "Usually takes the phone company about a week and a half to get over here."

"Don't trouble yourself on my account." Her smile was as smooth as her liquid voice. "I'll use a phone at Castillo House."

He stuffed the last letter in the filing cabinet and pushed it shut, then sat back in his chair, lifting one leg to the corner of his desk and linking his hands behind his head. She'd taken a few steps inside, her gaze moving around the square office.

"Seems a little…Andy Griffith."

"The whole world doesn't operate like your dad's precinct did."

Her lashes swept down, hiding her expression. He didn't want to wonder what her eyes contained. White-caps at his mention of her dad, or pools of quiet despair?

He wondered, anyway.

Her fingers slid along the length of the wood surface of the empty desk near the door.

He lowered his leg and sat forward. Picked up a paper clip lying inside the empty file folder and proceeded to mangle it. Hell. "How is your dad, anyway?" He'd never had much argument with Randall, except when it came to the man's stilted relationship with Delaney.

She didn't answer immediately. She folded her hands together in front of her, studied the inexpert seascape hanging on the wall. "He's in a care center now, actually."

Hell *and* damnation. He bent the paper clip so hard it snapped in two. He knew better than to offer any other kind of concern. She would rebuff it. He'd get mad.

They'd be right back in that familiar cycle.

"What happened?" he asked.

"He's had a few strokes this past year."

"A few." She adored her father but Randall Townsend pretty much ignored her, far as Sam was concerned. He'd been so busy mourning his son, he'd forgotten that his daughter was alive and well. "What's his condition?"

"Diminished mobility and speech." She dashed her hand over her tied-back hair, her gaze bouncing from the painting over the rest of the interior, landing on him, then skipping away. "He's pretty frustrated," she added after a moment.

"I'll bet. Your dad wouldn't like being thwarted by anything, particularly his own body."

"Yes." She smoothed her hair again. "Doesn't help that he refuses his meds."

She was nervous.

Too much of him wanted to ease that for her. Too much of him enjoyed seeing her rattled.

He was a head case. How suitable that he was still married to a psychiatrist.

He stood and headed toward her, perfectly aware of the little start she gave. "Come on."

"Where?" Suspicion glinted.

"You wanted to go to Castillo House, didn't you?"

"Yes." She moistened her lips, leaving a faint glisten behind that he looked at longer than was good for him.

Reach for the door, Vega.

But he just stood there, looking down at her. The air was suddenly thick and it didn't have squat to do with the past. It was real, and it was right now.

A pool of color rode her sculpted cheekbones, and her blue eyes went dark. He heard her breath. Soft. Unsteady.

His body tightened. He could reach for the door. Just put out his arm. Flip the lock.

"Sam."

Had he imagined the way she sighed his name?

Probably. There were enough nights his sleep was haunted with it.

Her slender, lovely throat worked in a swallow. He knew how the hollow at the base would taste. How he'd feel the flutter of her heartbeat there.

She moistened her lips again. Her eyes widened a little, as if she'd divined his thoughts.

He lifted his hand.

The door right beside them rattled. The blinds swayed.

He stifled an oath, and Delaney jumped two feet back, her gaze skittering away from his.

Then the door opened, and his grandmother stood there.

"Well," she snapped, thumping her cane on the ground, her bright brown eyes taking in the pair of them. "Is this her?"

Chapter 6

Sam let out a long breath. "Etta, what are you doing here?"

"I'd think that was obvious, Samson." She strode into the office, pushing him out of the way. "Since you won't bring your wife to meet me, I have to track you down to meet her. Have to hear from Sophie that you're parading her through town, even." She stopped in front of Delaney, looking her up and down.

But Delaney was no slouch in that department and she eyed Etta right back, apparently recovering her equilibrium easily enough. Or else she was covering it over with that particular skill she'd developed as the child of a society princess and an autocratic cop.

"New York, hmm?" Etta's voice was sharp.

Delaney raised her eyebrow. "Southern California?"

Sam nearly laughed, the surprise on Etta's face was so clear. "Don't get yourself riled up, Etta, or I'll have to call Dr. Hugo over to check your blood pressure."

Etta's head turned away from him, her steel-gray hair wound in a braid atop her head like some sort of crown. "He thinks he's being smart," she said to Delaney.

"He often does," she agreed mildly.

"Men." Etta thumped her cane on the tile floor for emphasis. "They all need a decent woman to keep them on the straight and narrow. Are you a decent woman?"

Now it was Delaney's turn to look surprised. Although if he didn't know her expressions as well as he did, he would have missed it. "I try to be," she murmured. "But Sam hardly needs—"

"Bah." Etta stepped forward until her braid was inches from knocking into Delaney's chin. She studied her closely. "At least you're old enough to know your own mind. Not some young thing still wet behind the ears."

"Mmm. Thank you?" Delaney's voice was a little faint.

"You'll come to Sunday dinner today," she announced. "We all eat together on Sundays, though Samson's got some idea he's going to miss it. And you can meet my son, Danté. Samson's father. His wife wasn't the decent sort. If she had been, he wouldn't have been so unfortunate—"

"Etta." Sam wrapped his hand firmly, gently, around his grandmother's arm. "Enough."

Her eyes flashed at him. "Enough, you say? What do you know about what's enough? You, who keeps your marriage a secret from your very own family. If I could reach them, I'd box your ears the way I used to when you were a misbehaving pup."

She turned back to Delaney. "You'll come to dinner and you'll tell us all about the wedding. Was it a church wedding, at least? I never thought I'd thank the day that Danté and that good-for-nothing had Sam on the mainland, but I do now. Otherwise we'd have to contend with the curse, too."

Through her veneer of composure, he thought Delaney was starting to look a little shell-shocked. "Curse?" Her gaze met his over Etta's head.

"The Turnabout curse, of course. Sam, haven't you told this poor girl *any*thing?"

There was no answer he could give without hurting Etta's feelings more than they already were. "The Turnabout curse says that anyone born on the island will only find happiness with someone else born on the island."

"But why?"

"Because the Castillo family always was trouble," Etta said firmly. "Good riddance to them, I say. I'm glad they're all gone now, though Caroline—the last one— wasn't so bad. But the Castillo people started the trouble more than a century ago, and it's been so ever since. Turns, which is what the natives are called, don't mix. Not well. Why, look at your poor father, Samson. He—"

"Made his own choices, Etta." He didn't want to get into this discussion. Not now. Not ever.

"—married a girl from the Midwest." Etta didn't miss a beat. "She never fit in. Led him a merry chase.

If it hadn't been for her, Danté never would have gotten involved with the Castillo family."

"Delaney isn't interested in all that," Sam warned.

Etta's lips narrowed into a thin, displeased line. "Fine, then. Ignore your family. Pretend we don't exist. You think that's going to change anything? You'll still know we're here, same as always."

She deliberately turned back to Delaney. "I don't suppose you have wedding pictures do you? No, probably not. I heard you arrived with only one small suitcase when you brought that boy with the odd name to Annie and Logan. Now why on earth they couldn't name their little program something more suitable than Castillo House I'll never know. They're not from the Castillo family, after all. Not at all. Logan is a Drake, and the Drakes go back nearly as long on the island as the Fieldings and our own Vega family does. Just seems strange to me. Did ever since I heard that they'd managed to buy up that property and restore the house. It was nearly a ruin, you know. But they worked hard, and look at all they've done in such a short time. That's because Logan has a decent woman by his side now. Annie. Well, there's some talk about her past, but everyone knows she's a good person."

Sam looked to the ceiling as his grandmother rattled on. And on.

Wedding pictures? Not likely. There had been a photographer at the Moonlight Chapel of Love all right. All set to shoot whatever package the happy couple selected from the laminated sign hanging on the wall inside the entrance. But Delaney had waved off the idea of any photographs, and he'd been more anxious to get to the honeymoon than to stand there and smile for the skinny, balding guy wearing a checked suit and an enormous camera.

Anxious for the honeymoon part because it was only when he had Delaney naked against him that he wasn't braced for her to change her mind about what they were doing. Convincing her to marry him at all had taken more fast, persuasive talking than he'd known he possessed.

"Etta." His voice was abrupt, brooking no argument. "We were on our way to Castillo House."

Etta's nonstop words trailed off. At last. She lifted her chin. "All right, then. Stubborn cuss. Was born that way and never changed. Well—" she held out her arms to Delaney "—give an old woman a hug, and you can be on your way."

He half expected Delaney to finagle her way out of that one. Her small smile was ragged around the fringes, but she leaned down and hugged Etta.

As she left, her cane thumping, even though he knew good and well she didn't really need the thing to walk, Etta did not demand a hug from Sam. Just one more method of expressing her displeasure where he was concerned.

Through the narrow blinds, he watched her cross the sidewalk and climb—nimbly, since she figured she wasn't being observed—into her blinding-white golf cart that Leo had fixed up for her the year before.

"I ought to write her a speeding ticket," he said when she shot down the street like a bat out of hell. He'd have to talk to Leo about toning down the cart's power. And maybe her interference was annoying, but it had kept him from doing something stupid.

Like trying to seduce the woman who didn't want to still be his wife.

"I liked her."

"You also like manic depressives, schizophrenics and general crazies."

"She clearly loves you."

Sam grunted and held open the door. "So do the mosquitoes when the humidity is high."

"I never knew my grandparents."

He locked the door and headed for the truck. "I remember."

Her eyes were pensive, a small line forming between her eyebrows. "You should go to dinner, Sam. You don't need to miss it on my account."

"I'm not."

"Then why?"

"Is that still one of your favorite questions, Delaney? *Why?* Why do you think you feel this way, patient X? Why do you think you chose to do this, or that, or the other? Why did you try to jump out of a moving car? Why is that particular dream bothering you?"

"You're avoiding the answer."

"Yeah, and I didn't even need a medical degree to figure that out."

The line between her eyes deepened as her expression tightened. "Was there ever anything about me that you actually liked, Sam? You hated my practice, my patients, and the hours that I put in."

"I didn't hate your practice or your patients." Do-Wright? That might be another story.

"Your actions said otherwise."

"My actions?" He didn't care that they were standing right there in the middle of town for anyone and their brother to see or hear. "What actions would those be, Delaney? Wanting you to scale back your hours to a simple full-time week? Forty hours instead of seventy. And seventy was a good week, because sometimes it was more."

"You worked long hours, too, Sam."

He'd thought he'd dealt with it. But the emotion came up from somewhere deep inside. "I wasn't the one who was pregnant."

She whitened and her eyes looked like bruised sapphires. "Too bad you weren't," she said huskily. "Not only would you be a medical marvel, but you probably wouldn't have lost the baby, either."

And there it was.

The thing that neither one of them had openly acknowledged in twenty-one long months.

"You've blamed me all along for what happened, Sam. I know that. But trust me. You can't blame me more than I blame myself."

"Blame." The word tasted vile. "You don't know the meaning of blame. And you brought Alonso here. That's a helluva note, Delaney. What did you want to do?

Really stick it to me? Rub it in my face every time I might happen to see the kid? Is that your payback?"

"Payback for what?" Her voice rose. "Alonso was no more responsible for the car accident that night than you were."

Right. "It was three o'clock in the damned morning, Delaney. If the kid was out of his house at that time it was his mother's responsibility, not yours."

"Maria had no way to get to him. I had a car—"

"Which you drove about twice a year."

"—and I knew if I called the *police* for help, Alonso would probably get taken into custody again simply because of the people he was with!"

In other words, she hadn't asked *him* because he'd have done just what she suspected. "Why was he with them, Delaney? Because he was just like them." He had to believe it or his own actions would be even more intolerable.

"No." She shook her head. "He wasn't. But you never took the time to find that out. All you saw him as was a tool—a means to help you nail his father's killer. You said yourself that Anton was a sleaze, but even a sleaze didn't deserve to be murdered. Well, Alonso was just a boy. He wasn't Anton. He was only eleven years old when all that happened. And in those two years before I…we…before we became personally involved, you never stopped seeing him as anything but a lead in your very cold case. Even after we got married. Until the accident." Her voice strangled to a halt.

He never had nailed Anton's killer. Killers, as he'd

deduced in the end. A trio of individuals who'd managed to get out of the country well before his life blew up in his face. He'd failed there, too.

He yanked open the passenger door. "Get in."

"That's it? That's all you have to say."

"You wanted to go to Castillo House. Get in."

She looked ready to argue. But after a moment, she climbed up on the seat, the lure of an opportunity to speak to Do-Wright evidently too great to deny.

They didn't speak as he drove out to the southern tip of the island where the big house sat like the lord of the manor. Majestic, white stuccoed walls, pitch-black wood beams and windows at every turn, the enormous house was by far the largest, finest structure on the island. The gates at the end of the driveway were open as usual. Even though the kids there came from all manner of troubled backgrounds, Castillo House wasn't a detention facility. The gravel crunched under his tires as he stopped. Thin rays of sunlight slanted across the tiled roof of the house that had become the unlikely home to an unlikely mix of people.

Delaney barely cast him a look before she slid from the vehicle and nearly ran up the wide steps and disappeared through the front door.

Then he drove away.

But the memories drove right alongside him.

Sam had never met a hospital that he liked. And this one was definitely no exception.

He stopped, his hand pressed flat against the hospital

door. He could see the foot of the bed and the barely there bump where her feet were covered by the rigidly tucked bedding.

The hard edges of the door dug into his palm.

Once her feet were warm enough, Delaney always worked the toes of one foot from beneath the bedding after she was asleep. Her unconscious thermostat. Before then, her feet were always chilly.

"You can go on in." A young nurse—all smiles and bouncy brown hair—nodded at him as she rolled a clear-sided bassinet down the hall. "Your wife's been waiting for you."

Waiting.

The nurse smiled again, oblivious that her cheerful encouragement was a damning indictment.

He widened the opening and stepped past the door.

She was lying on her side, facing away from him. Her hair lay limp against the thin white pillow beneath her head.

He walked into the small room and rounded the foot of the bed. Her eyes were open, pools of pale blue that followed his progress as he dragged the side chair close to the bed.

He sat. Looked into those blue eyes of hers. "Are you all right?" Stupid question. The damage went far deeper than the cut on her forehead.

"I'm being released tomorrow." Her voice was quiet. Calm. Too calm. He'd have felt better if she'd raged. But she wasn't one to rage.

"Good."

Her hand lay atop the thin blue blanket. Fingers barely curving downward against the mattress. He started to reach for it. But her fingers curled tighter. Barely noticeable, but still a retreat from him. He continued lifting his hand and shoved it, instead, through his hair.

He looked around the antiseptic hospital room. "Are you in pain?" He looked back in time to see the faint movements at the corner of her lips. A frown.

"No."

Not anymore. When he'd been called to the hospital the night the accident happened, she'd been curled in a ball of agony. Too tightly coiled to accept comfort of any type. Not from the doctor who'd wanted to sedate her; not from him, who'd wanted to hold her.

She wasn't the only one who'd lost something two days ago in the accident that had torn her rarely driven sedan into scrap metal. Given the severity of the collision, he'd been grateful her injuries hadn't been considerably worse.

She could have died.

His stomach was still in a knot.

"My doctor said he called you."

He nodded, though her words were more statement than question. "He told me." His throat ached. He focused on her hand with its protectively curled fingers.

Her eyes closed for a moment. When she opened them, her gaze didn't meet his. "I thought you'd be here earlier."

"I'm sorry."

Her distant expression rejected the apology. He closed his mind yet again to the thoughts of the accident. The reason she'd been out at all at that time of night, in that area of town. "Internal Affairs called me in this morning."

That, at least, caused her gaze to slide his way. "Why?"

He should have kept his mouth shut. Waited to tell her. There'd been a lot of things he'd done wrong. This was just one more.

"Samson?" her soft voice prompted.

He exhaled slowly. Deliberately letting go of the fury that still shook him. Instead of being by his wife's side when she'd heard the final news that her pregnancy couldn't be saved, he'd been defending his professional integrity. "Some evidence has gone missing from one of my cases. They wanted to know if I had something to do with it."

Of course you didn't. He waited for her automatic rejection of the idea. The waiting went on seconds, minutes, eons too long.

"Did you?"

He sat back in the chair, absorbing that as the gulf between them widened. Her lashes lowered for a long moment.

Tears, he thought. She hated them.

He exhaled roughly and leaned forward again, arms braced on his thighs. "Are you sure you're not in pain?" Because he couldn't help himself, he reached out. Smoothed the hair from her forehead, away from the bandage.

Her eyes opened finally, but she didn't meet his gaze. "I'm fine," she said eventually.

But they both knew that for the lie it was.

She wasn't fine. He wasn't fine. *They* weren't fine. Maybe it was time they faced it.

Sam sighed, heading off the road when he saw Winnie Haggerty waving madly at him. But even as duty called, his thoughts were on that time, nearly two years ago.

The day after the doctor had confirmed the baby was gone, Delaney returned home. The day after that, she was back at work. The bandage on her forehead was replaced by a narrow strip. Barely noticeable when she parted her hair differently. But the damage had been done. Only a portion of it caused by an accident that should never have happened.

The rest of the damage, he knew, rested squarely in their own hands.

Two weeks after her release from the hospital, he'd moved out.

Chapter 7

"What do you mean she's gone?" Sam squinted against the sunlight that speared through the gathering clouds. "I dropped off Delaney hours ago."

Annie sat back on her heels, a small gardening spade in her hand. Her eyes rested on his face for a moment, probably taking in the welt he'd gotten from getting in the way of Vern trying to pummel his brother. But she didn't comment on it. "I'm sorry, Sam. Delaney visited briefly with Alonso, then left." Her head whipped around at a movement beside her. Two of her charges hefted a large flat of plants. "The marigolds go over by the steps," she instructed, pointing with the spade.

She waited long enough to be sure her request was

heeded, then looked back up at Sam. "She might have told Alonso where she was heading. He's around here somewhere if you want to talk to him."

The last person Sam had any desire to talk to was Alonso Petrofski. "Thanks, Annie."

"If you can't find him, check with Logan. But I'll warn you now, if he sees you, he's probably going to draft you into helping him with some wiring he's doing."

Any other day he'd have freely volunteered his help. "I'll find him," he said, and turned from Annie and her little troop of gardeners. If there really was supposed to be healing in the art of gardening, he'd have to say Castillo House was proof of it. For generations the earth hadn't had the ability to support a single plant. Now, with Annie and Logan at the helm, and their youthful charges working at it, the grounds around Castillo House were beginning to flourish.

A mutual case of the earth healing the people and the people healing the earth.

Delaney had brought Alonso here.

They'd be lucky if Castillo House—nearly fully restored thanks to the mountain of money sunk into it— was still standing when the kid was finished.

Sam found the tall boy on the half-size basketball court he'd helped Logan lay out the year before. Sitting, balanced, on a basketball, his long legs splayed while he talked with Caitlin. The pregnant girl.

When both of the teens saw him, twin expressions of defiance and dislike came over their faces. Sam had nothing against Caitlin—had never had much encounter with her at all. But where Alonso was concerned, the dislike was mutual. "Where's Delaney?"

"Dude. How should I know?"

"She came to talk to you."

Alonso shrugged. He shared a look with Caitlin.

"Did you upset her?"

"That ain't my job, man. It's what you do."

"Did she say where she was going?"

Alonso shrugged again.

Sam crouched down, getting in the kid's face. "*Dude*. What'd she say?"

Alonso jerked back, but at least the scorn left his face. "Goodbye," he said flatly. "She said goodbye. Again. Like she did last night. That tell you anything important?"

Sam straightened. "Watch yourself here, Alonso. I'm the only law around. No liberal-minded judge on hand at a moment's notice to keep your tail out of the sling. Cross one line of legality and you'll be sitting in *my* jail cell for the three weeks it takes for the judge to come calling."

As he was walking away, he heard Caitlin's whisper. "See? I told you Logan was a walk in the park compared to the sheriff."

He ignored the observation. After enough years on the force in New York, he didn't expect to be loved by the public. But his mind was on what Alonso said. It shouldn't matter that Delaney told Alonso goodbye. She couldn't go off-island without him knowing about it.

Still, he drove from one end of Turnabout to the other. Avoided looking at Etta's house as he passed it.

They'd all be sitting down to dinner by now, acting as if the prodigal father had finally returned.

There was no sign of Delaney.

He drove down to the dock. She'd told Alonso goodbye. After a long while he turned away from the emptiness of the ocean stretched before him and headed back to the emptiness of home.

Delaney carefully hung up the phone and sat there, looking at it where it rested on Sam's granite countertop. She needn't have worried about him being nearby when she made the necessary call to Chad; he'd been absent since she'd returned from seeing Alonso. Her idea of using a phone at Castillo House had been nixed because Logan had been doing some rewiring.

"Life on the island," Annie had said with a shrug when Delaney learned that bit of news. It was a refrain she suspected the residents had to repeat frequently.

She had, in not terribly flattering terms, when she'd walked all the way back to Sam's place. She'd refused Annie's offer of a ride, knowing the woman's day was already busy enough.

The silence pressed in on her, and she slid her fingers over the cool surface of the phone. Toyed with the cord.

Sam's absence was a good thing, she reminded herself. She could just imagine what kind of comments he'd have had to make if he'd come in while she was talking to Chad.

Understandably, Chad had been upset.

For years—even before the collision of Sam in her

life—Chad had made it plain that he cared for her. Then, after Sam left, he'd started in again. But only recently had she finally agreed to seriously consider marrying him. They worked well together. They had common ideals, common tastes. She *liked* the calm, sane relationship they had. She *liked* knowing what to expect and knowing that whatever Chad did would never tear her soul in two.

But, even after she'd told him she couldn't marry him…and *why*…he'd never lost his temper. Never raised his voice. He'd simply calmly, reasonably, assured her that he had their practice well in hand and she should take her time. Once she'd dealt with Sam and handled the legalities to completion, they would revisit the matter.

Revisit the matter.

Hardly an impassioned response.

Which you don't want anyway, right?

She shook her head and reached for the phone again, punching out her father's number at the hospital care center. He answered on the second ring. Their conversation was woefully brief.

She wouldn't have minded talking longer.

Randall Townsend didn't like to talk at all. It used to be only her he'd tended to shut out of meaningful conversation. Now, with his speech so difficult, he shut out nearly everyone.

She propped her head in her hand, staring blindly at the glass bowl of seeds sitting by the phone. She was a grown woman. Yet she still wanted her father's approval.

Might as well wish for the moon, Laney. You'll get it easier.

"Problems between the lovebirds?"

She jerked, her nerves jangling. The man moved like a cat, even with those scuffed boots of his. "It's rude to sneak up on people. I'd have thought your grandmother would have taught you that."

"It's my house. And you need to keep your nose out of my family's business." Sam entered the kitchen more fully.

Then she saw the bruise on his face. She slid off the bar stool and hurried toward him, the sting of his warning taking a back seat, alongside the baggage of their shared past. "God. Sam. What happened?"

He shrugged off her tentative touch. "Two fools named Haggerty who seem intent on pushing each other off a cliff."

Delaney's hands fell back to her sides. She watched him pull out the ever-popular bag of frozen peas and press it over his eye.

Then he turned and looked at her. "I thought you'd left."

"I wish I had." Her stomach flip-flopped. "All the charter services I called in San Diego were booked solid. So, I guess I'm not inventive enough to figure a way off the island other than Mr. Montoya's ferry. I still can't believe nobody else on this island owns a proper boat."

"Not one that'll handle the crossing well."

"Yes. I realize that." Particularly after she'd thoroughly questioned Annie and Logan Drake on that point. She crossed her arms. "Does it hurt?"

Sam's gaze narrowed. "If I said yes, are you going to kiss it better?"

"Don't be clichéd."

"I'll take that as a no." His tone was odd as he moved past her to slide open the glass door to the deck, scooping up a handful of seeds from the bowl before stepping outside.

It took Delaney a moment to realize that it was the lack of mocking in his voice that was odd.

She followed him. Hovered next to the glass door as he tossed the seeds far beyond the rail. Seagulls and a host of other birds she couldn't identify immediately dove, their songs raucous.

His hands closed over the wooden rail, his head lowered for a moment. The frozen bag sitting on the rail seemed forgotten. "Why'd you bring Petrofski here, Delaney?"

She tried not to bristle. "Does he have something to do with the bruise you're sporting?" He'd have a black eye by morning.

Sam didn't look her way. "If he did, he'd be sitting in my jail cell."

"So, who is?"

He sighed sharply. "Nobody."

"You took a punch and didn't lock somebody up?"

He angled a look her way. "Why bring him, Delaney?"

Naturally he wouldn't be deterred from that. "I've told you that you're too hard on him. Yes, he's shown some bad judgment, but that was years ago, and he's paid the price. For heaven's sake, his mother died last year."

"Whatever."

"I can't believe you are so unsympathetic toward him! Your mother died when you were young, didn't she?" The mother that Etta claimed to be no-good and not decent.

He finally turned. "Yes and it's not the same."

"Only because you're too stubborn to see otherwise."

"And you're gullible."

"Well. As usual, I appreciate your vote of confidence in my professional abilities. Nice to know that some things haven't changed. You still think I'm a fool."

"You have no objectivity where he's concerned. You never did. Not about Alonso. Not about your brother. Not about your father."

"Neither my brother nor my father have *anything* to do with Alonso."

"It was your dad who assigned me to Anton's murder investigation," he reminded.

"So?"

"So, sixteen years ago—before he got pulled back into the Russian mob—Anton was your mother's gardener at that big, fancy estate of hers."

She could feel the hard plane of the glass door pressing against her spine. Sixteen years ago she and her mother hadn't been speaking. "So?"

"So, what do you think Anton and Jessica were doing together? Pruning rosebushes? Come on, Delaney. They were lovers. You know that."

"What if I do? She and my father had been divorced by then for years. She was a free woman. It didn't matter to anyone what she did."

"Mattered to you. You hadn't been able to save Randy from himself and the drugs and booze and larceny he got into. But you're determined to save Alonso—a kid who could easily have been your own brother if Jessica hadn't tired of trysting in the gardener's toolshed."

Delaney blinked, absorbing that. "That's quite a leap of logic, Sam." She managed a respectable touch of lightness. "When did you come to such lofty conclusions?"

There was nothing light in his tone. "I've had nearly two bloody years to think about it. So how'd Do-Wright take the news? You did call him, I assume."

"He was understanding." She'd choke before she'd tell about Chad's "revisit the matter" comment. Sam would have a field day with that. "That cold bag isn't going to do your eye any good unless you use it."

He closed his hand over the peas and threw them—hard—onto a padded chair.

She jumped.

"What's he do for you, Delaney? Were you already sleeping with him before I left?"

"No! I told you we're not—" She caught the gleam in his eyes, and anger shored up her own spine. "I never broke my vows." Even when she'd thought they were divorced. "Can you say the same?"

A muscle ticked in his jaw. "Would it matter? You've already tried divorcing me once. Only a matter of time before you take care of that detail."

Fury bubbled inside her. "Well, you didn't, and you were the one who walked out. What would you have me do, Sam? Stay married forever to a man who doesn't want to *be* with me?" She realized with a sort of removed surprise that she was shaking. "So maybe I *do* want to marry Chad. At least he's steady and reliable and—"

"Trustworthy? Honest?"

A single raindrop fell between them. It landed with a heavy plop on the redwood deck.

"I never said you weren't honest."

"You just believed I was capable of stealing evidence. It was money, you know. Counterfeit as all hell, but it was in Anton's effects that we seized after his death."

She *hadn't* known that. "I never believed that you'd stolen anything." She'd barely been functioning back then.

His lips twisted. The past loomed over them, as oppressive as the clouds had become. "Is *he?* Honest?"

"Chad won't hurt me," Delaney finally said. How could he? She'd never put her heart in his hands the way she'd done with Sam. She wouldn't be so foolish again.

He stepped closer, his boot covering the pearling splatter of that raindrop. "Do you love him?"

Her chin angled. She couldn't step back even if she'd tried. Thick panes of glass were at her back. "He's a good friend." He'd been there before Sam. And he'd been there after.

"But you haven't slept with him."

"A person might think you're jealous, considering the way you keep dwelling on that."

"You're my wife."

"Well, *you* weren't sleeping with me!" Her voice rang out. Her face flamed hot.

He leaned closer, one hand pressed against the glass above her head. "We could always get each other into bed. That was never the problem. It was living with each other that was the problem."

She tried to deny it, but words wouldn't come.

"I wanted it all with you," he said flatly. "You wanted nothing to change. Except that you'd have someone to keep your feet warm at night. I was *your* gardener, Delaney. And as soon as I wanted more with you than a toolshed—things like a house outside the city, a couple of kids—you froze me out."

"That is *not* true."

"You put your career, Alonso, between us every chance you got. Hell, when we get right down to it, you never really wanted to get married in the first place." He drew his finger down her neck. "You only agreed because you were pregnant."

He'd only asked because she'd been pregnant. "Considering what a poor wife I was, *you* could have done something when those papers came back from the court."

"One would think," he murmured.

"Then you could marry someone like S-Sara Drake."

"True enough."

Her throat ached. "So you admit it. You are involved with her."

"She's a good friend," he said deliberately.

A raindrop fell on her forehead. "Sometimes I really hate you, Sam."

"Guess that's better than nothing," he muttered.

She put her hands on his shoulders, intending to push him away.

Then he brushed his lips over hers.

Once.

Twice.

Her heart kicked up in her throat, and her stomach hollowed out. And instead of pushing, her fingers curled, suddenly clinging.

He caught her chin in his hand, tilting her head. "Open your mouth, dammit."

She stared into his eyes, seeing her own reflection.

And heaven help her, she opened her mouth.

She tasted his hiss of satisfaction. Felt the race of it in her blood. Then his mouth covered hers, his kiss deep. Hot. Sweet.

His arm slid behind her back, cushioning her against the unyielding glass door. But his hard body was no more yielding.

Raindrops fell on her face. Tears from heaven?

She tore her mouth away from his. "We can't do this."

He caught her chin, his gaze boring into hers. "You mean you won't."

"We're adults." She swallowed, giving up on regulating her uneven breath in favor of speech because she couldn't seem to master both. "Not teenagers ruled by hormones."

A raindrop hit her shoulder, and his fingers trailed over it, then along the vee of her shirt. Down, down, and up again. Her nerves jumped and her skin felt too tight.

"It's still there." Sam's voice was a low rasp.

She couldn't press her spine flatter—not with his hand at her back preventing it. "What?"

He lowered his head. His hard cheek brushed hers. "Heat." His breath teased her ear. "Same as before."

She squared her shoulders with an effort. "Are you trying to live in the past, Sam? That's a dangerous endeavor."

"Remember the couch incident? Your office. Late that one night. Chinese takeout. A soft leather couch."

"Incident." Her voice was choked. "Lovely. So romantic."

"Is that what you get from Do-Wright?" He skimmed his thumb down the vee again, then beyond, gliding over the hard push of her nipple through the thin fabric. "He's just sweetly romancing you right up the wedding aisle?"

Her skin burned. Not from his words, but his marauding fingertip. "No, that's what *you* did." She pushed at his shoulders, but he was immovable.

"Did I romance you, Delaney?"

She felt the gentle tug of his teeth on her earlobe, and the clouds overhead seemed to whirl. "Sam…"

"It was hot," he whispered. "It's still hot." His hand was suddenly at the hem of her shirt, drawing it upward. "Tell me I'm wrong. Tell me to stop, Delaney. Tell me your body isn't crying for this. For us."

She threw back her head, but the words to blast his arrogant assurance wouldn't rise. His hand at her back pressed her, arching, against him.

"Nobody will ever fit either one of us better than this." He cupped her hip, his fingers kneading.

"Sex." The word burst from her. "It's only…oh—" he'd slid down the side zipper of her slacks "—only sex." Except nothing with Sam had ever been "only."

His head dipped. His mouth covered her shoulder where he'd tugged aside the neckline. "Take down your hair."

"No." What was *wrong* with her? Five minutes ago she'd been defending another man. Another raindrop fell, catching on her cheek. "I don't want to do this."

He suddenly straightened. Pulled his hand from the small of her back. From the edge of her panties. He took a step back.

His shirt was half-off, his hair ruffled. From the breeze or her fingers?

He lifted his hands to the sides. "Now what? Your choice, Delaney. Walk away."

The way he had? Her eyes suddenly burned.

This man was one of the most truly dangerous things she'd ever encountered in her life. The first had been a cliff her inebriated brother had driven them off one cold dark night. To her father's grief, she'd been the one to survive.

Had she survived Sam?

Her heart thudded heavily, in tempo with some elemental song that had always played between them. Was there a point in denying it? In continuing to pretend that she could ever be satisfied with the lukewarm emotion inspired by anyone else?

She was a fool.

She was an unwanted wife. Thorny and uncompromising.

But if she didn't get Sam's hands back on her, right now, she'd go stark-raving mad. What was survival when her soul yearned for something it had already lost?

She stepped forward and caught his hand in hers. Guided it down to her breast and pressed it there. Sensation cramped through her, and she lifted her mouth until it found his.

"This doesn't change anything." Her voice was hoarse.

"I don't care."

His fingers worked between their bodies, and in seconds he'd pulled her shirt over her head. Tossed it to the deck.

The warm rain fell harder, sliding down her bare shoulders. His hands were even warmer when they covered her bare breasts. Her flesh seemed to swell. She exhaled, a moan in her throat. "Sam—"

"Take down your hair." His voice was hoarse now, too. Filled with the same kind of madness she felt.

She lifted her hands. Her breasts pushed harder against his palms. She fumbled at the twist in her hair. Dragged at the pins, letting them fall. Her hair unrolled, caught by the balmy damp breeze.

He exhaled, his expression fierce. "Now put your hands on me."

Bossy. That's what he was. Bossy. Controlling.

She reached for him again, dragged at the hem of his T-shirt and thrust her hands beneath it, feeling the searing heat of his tight flesh, the rasp of silky-crisp chest hair. She slid her hands over his shoulders, taking the shirt with them. Pressed her torso against his.

A soft cry rose in her throat. It was drowned out by the cry of birds still diving for the seeds that Sam had tossed. His arm behind her back was an iron railing of its own. She was barely aware of the rain when he lifted her against him, pushed her back once more against the glass. And too acutely aware of his belt buckle digging into her stomach.

Neither made a move to find dryer ground. Her hands fairly attacked his belt buckle and the button fly beneath it. He'd always worn the same kind of jeans. Used to tease her over her impatience at unfastening the buttons. Now she slid her fingers into his waist and yanked. The jeans popped open.

Sam laughed soundlessly against her neck. But his laughter turned to a groan when her trembling fingers delved beneath the denim. He exhaled roughly, then his own hands were as busy as hers. Ridding his jeans once and for all. Sliding her narrow pants down, over her thighs, off her feet, then tossing them aside.

"Those are silk," she said faintly.

He reached for her. "You're silkier." His mouth found her hip bone.

Her throat was tight, her need a hiss between her teeth. On the verge of begging, she gasped when he tore her panties and rose, then slid his hands around her thighs and lifted her, even as his weight pinned her against the door.

"Now?" His eyes were hot. Bossy, yes, but even now, he'd stop.

She buried her face in the crook of his neck. "Now."

"Look at me," he insisted.

Delaney twined her arms tighter around his shoulders, burying her face deeper. Her mouth opened against him, tasting raindrops and warm, hard flesh. She writhed against him, need streaking through her.

"Look at me." His voice was rougher, his hands like irons on her, pressing her back against the window, preventing her from moving against him, when moving and taking was all she wanted.

An agony of frustration coiled in her.

She pushed her fingers through his hair. Would have pulled if it weren't so short.

Begging was not beyond her, after all. "Please."

"Look…at…me."

She threw back her head, her gaze racing over his face. A man she knew, yet didn't. A man who'd been part of her but had held himself apart. "Did you start this just to torment me?"

Between narrowed lashes his eyes gleamed rich brown. The bruise high on his cheekbone made him look even more darkly dangerous. "I want you to look at my face and know who I am."

Edgy tremors quaked deep inside her. No arguments came to her lips. No bristling emotion against his bottom-line attitude. She'd always fallen prey to the blinding chemistry between them. Even after all this time, nothing had changed.

"I know who you are, Sam. I've always known." She sounded as if she'd just run a marathon. "Now. Please." She pressed her forehead against his jaw, her hands cradling his head. "Please."

He exhaled sharply, and he took her.

She cried out, wrapped her legs around his hard hips. The glass behind her shook. She didn't care. It had been so long.

The rain fell harder. Her hands slipped over his wet skin. Everything inside her tightened.

Sam groaned and suddenly moved, carrying her to the cushioned chaise. His mouth covered hers and he thrust clear to the heart of her.

She had the faintest thought that they were giving the seagulls quite an eyeful.

Then she couldn't think anymore.

She could only feel.

The warm rain. Sam.

And unbearable pleasure as their world splintered around them.

Chapter 8

Delaney woke to the feel of a blast furnace against her back and the warmth of sunshine on her face. The moment she moved, Sam slid his arm over her waist, his hand an instinctive arrow straight to her breast.

Hardly daring to breathe, she turned her head.

His hooded gaze met hers.

She'd told him nothing would change, yet she felt herself having to cling to that belief. The past was over. It couldn't be undone. Not the bad, nor the good.

And there *had* been good.

Until the blame had set in, eating them alive.

He threaded his fingers through her hair, spreading it out across the pillow. "Stop thinking so hard."

She couldn't bear the weight of his gaze and looked

away. Through the sliding glass door she could see the lumps of their clothing still heaped on the deck. "It's when I stop thinking that things get so messed up." She covered her mouth with her fingers for a moment. She could no more stop thinking than she could stop wanting what wasn't meant to be. "I didn't know about the divorce, Sam. I swear it. I'm sorry."

He bent his arm, propping his head up on his hand. "I believe you."

"The attorney I used was a patient. I know it was stupid," she said hurriedly at his telling expression, "but he needed so badly to prove to himself that he was competent. He'd been fired so many—"

"Jeez, Delaney." He rolled on his back, laying his arm over his eyes.

The movement threw his abs into sharp definition and the blanket over his hips perilously dipped. Realizing her gaze was lingering, she quickly looked down at the sheet, tucking it around herself. The last thing she needed was to be caught drooling over her estranged husband's most excellent physique.

"Do you think you can save the world one patient at a time?" His voice had gone tight, reminiscent of so many similar times. "It's not up to you to solve their every problem."

She clutched the sheet to her and sat up. "I know that." How easy they fell into their usual pattern. "But not every patient of mine has a physiological problem. Sometimes it's circumstances. Surroundings—"

"Like Alonso?" His voice went terse.

"Yes, like Alonso. He's trying so hard, Sam. He's doing well in school again. He's not drinking. Or smoking. Anything."

"Then why bring him here if he's so perfect?"

"Because he needs a home away from his old gang. You know how hard it is to break free from that life. And with his mother gone now—"

"It's a wonder you didn't just try to adopt him yourself." Sam threw back the sheet and climbed out of bed. "Then you'd have the kid you really want with no pregnancy at all."

She felt as if he'd slapped her. She quickly looked down. Not because Sam exhibited any modesty but because the display of all that bare flesh just seemed to hone the edge of her pain. "I wanted our baby, Sam."

She heard the rustle of denim, the snap of his jeans. "Right." His voice was grim. "All your actions were evidence of that. Wouldn't take time out of your schedule to buy maternity clothes. Wouldn't cut back on your hours even though the OB was warning you about your blood pressure."

She pleated the sheet between her fingers. And he'd only married her *because* of the baby. They'd been adults, but they'd acted as foolishly as teenagers, and in the end he'd blamed her for everything.

No more than she'd blamed herself.

"We're talking about Alonso," she managed after a long moment. "What he needs. And you just said it. I'm not an…an appropriate parental figure." She forged on despite his expression. Despite the fact that she felt mired in sucking mud. "I work too many hours. That's not what Alonso needs. It'd be wonderful if he had a *real* family. But that's not going to happen. And what Annie and Logan are doing at Castillo House is the next best thing. It *is* a perfect fit for him." She unconsciously leaned toward him, willing him to understand this at least.

"He's the only kid there still on probation for anything." His face was hard, the bruise on his cheekbone pronounced.

"For only two more months! Other than that, he's no different from any of those children. Troubled pasts of one sort or another. Homeless, bereaving. Unwitting victims to violence and destruction. Castillo House gives them a new start. A place to grow. Is it so wrong that I want that for a fifteen-year-old boy?"

"You sound like a walking brochure for the place. And he's not just *any* fifteen-year-old."

"I know." He was the reason she and Sam had ever met. And he was inextricably woven into the event that had been their final finish.

"And if it doesn't work out for him here? Turnabout is a place out of time, Delaney. He's used to the streets of New York."

Relief made it easier to talk. At least he'd left the topic of their lost baby. "Then I'll find another program for him. And another. I won't give up on him, Sam. I can't."

"Why? Why is *he* so damned important? You have to know that helping him doesn't change what happened to Randy."

"Because it's what I do, Sam. I help people. You do, too, just in a different way."

"But that doesn't entail traipsing across the entire country."

"Sometimes it does." She'd spent months searching for the right place for Alonso. "He was living in a halfway house with men twice his age or better. That was the best Social Services could do for him. But what he is is a kid who's lost both his parents."

"How'd Maria die?" His question was grudging.

"Uterine cancer. She was underinsured. I found out that Alonso was taking care of her once she became bedridden."

He ran his hand down his face, muffling an oath.

"He needs a home, Samson. I believe Annie and Logan will care for him. Provide the structure and security he needs. And Betty Weathers is the therapist they've got in-house. Have you met her? I have. A few times before we came here. She's top-notch. I think that being on this island—this place out of time—will allow him to find his own footing without danger of bad influences pulling him astray."

Sam listened to her impassioned voice. Watched her fierce expression. He'd always known it. That when she cared, when she believed in something—*someone*—nothing stood in her way for long.

But she hadn't believed in them. Not the marriage they'd had and certainly not in him. Not when the chips were down. When his entire precinct was whispering behind his back. When suspicion and accusation turned his way.

He'd spent half his lifetime—since he'd gone into law enforcement—fighting against the stigma of his heritage. Hell, it was Danté's first arrest that had driven Sam from one coast to the other. He'd gone as far as he could to distance himself. So he knew what it meant to cross the country in search of change. But it had still caught up to him, and he couldn't have shared it with the one person who'd ever really mattered. Because she'd been lying in a hospital bed, recovering from the miscarriage caused by an accident that *he* should have been man enough to prevent.

She hadn't believed in him, and she hadn't even known about his father. About what Danté was.

Her eyes were soft, serious. Her pale blond hair tumbled against her slender shoulders, and her soft lips looked rosy and swollen. She looked as if she'd spent the night making love, and he damned the fact that the sight moved him.

There weren't enough hours in the day to satisfy his craving where she was concerned. "I've got to get to the station," he said abruptly.

Her eyes flickered. She glanced at the clock on his nightstand. Did a double take.

At least she hadn't been clock watching.

She scrambled off the bed, dragging the sheet with her. "I missed the morning ferry, didn't I?"

He went still. Of course. Sex, as she'd said, wouldn't

change anything. Wouldn't steer her far from the course she'd set for herself.

"Yeah," he answered.

"Dandy. And the second run?"

"Around three. Maybe four depending on Diego's mood."

She swept up the sheet more fully. "I need a shower."

And he knew better than to suggest she share his.

He could persuade her to agree, but he'd be the one to have to live with the memory of it when she was long gone.

So he kept his mouth clamped shut as she hurried from the room with a rustle of sheeting. She turned back at the last minute. "You're not going to leave before I'm cleaned up, are you?"

That nasty trust thing again. But not unmerited. He'd considered doing just that. "You've got ten minutes," he said evenly.

She nodded and disappeared across the hall. He heard the door to his guest room close.

She made it in less than ten minutes. He was watering his plants when he heard the flap of her ugly pink sandals, and she appeared. Her hair was wet, pulled back again in a snug knot at the nape of her neck. She'd darkened her lashes and smeared gloss across her lips. Despite all that, and even though her suit—the one she'd arrived in—was a little wrinkled, she looked sleek and cool and *very* Delaney.

"I can drive you out to Castillo House or you can hang at Maisy's Place. She has an outdoor restaurant. The chef's pretty good."

"Castillo House."

He knew she had to be hungry by now, even after the midnight snack they'd shared. "Wouldn't want to pass up a chance to spend more time with your favorite delinquent."

Her eyes frosted. "Even after what I've told you, you say that."

"I remember taking him in for breaking and entering."

Her lips firmed. "I thought you were in a hurry."

He tipped the last of the water out over some green thing that Etta had promised him would live forever no matter how badly he treated it, and left the watering can on the hall table. "I am."

She stood pointedly near the door, then followed him outside. The sun was shining again, as if the rain from the previous day had never happened.

In fact, it was a postcard-perfect day. The kind that drew an increasing number of tourists to their little island. The shops in town could use the dollars, but often it meant a few more headaches for Sam. With strangers to the island tended to come mischief.

He drove down the length of the island and dropped her off in front of Castillo House. Once again Annie and their charges were outside. When he drove up, they all turned to see, Alonso included.

Delaney gathered her briefcase and reached for the door.

"Tell Logan you want to get Diego's last run. He'll make sure you make it."

Her gaze slid back to his. An odd curve hit her lips.

Disappointment? Unlikely.

"Well." She softly cleared her throat. "Okay. Um…"

"Use a better attorney this time." His voice was gruff. "Your mother's if you have to." Jessica might be many things, but she'd at least surrounded herself with a cadre of competent advisors.

Tears welled. Spilled over. One slid down her cheek. "Sam, I…this isn't what I intended."

Maybe it had been disappointment after all. "I know."

She bit her lip. Leaned forward suddenly and pressed her lips to his cheek. "Goodbye, Samson." Then she ducked her head and quickly climbed out of the truck. He saw her wipe her eyes as she hurried away.

He let out a long breath. Dredged up enough will-power to put the truck in Drive and hit the gas.

His mood was dark when he let himself into Etta's house several minutes later. She sat in her rocking chair, her nimble fingers working over whatever she was knitting. Probably another baby blanket that she would add to the pile she already had while bemoaning her lack of grandchildren. She didn't turn his way. Didn't greet him at all.

Still unhappy about his defection from dinner the day before.

"Where is he?"

She sniffed and ignored him.

He sighed and headed through to the kitchen. Spotted his father out in the backyard hunched over the old junker of a car that he'd brought home a long time ago before Sam was even old enough to drive.

He pushed out the rear door, letting the screen slap shut behind him.

Danté looked up. Squinted into the sunlight as he wiped the grease from his hands on a dingy red rag. "You're late."

"I was busy." He'd be damned if he'd apologize to Danté, or explain what he'd been doing. "Let's go."

Danté tossed aside the rag and silently followed him through the house. Etta was silent, too, as she watched them.

They climbed into Sam's truck. Danté fidgeted. Sam knew his old man wanted a smoke, just as Danté knew that he couldn't while he was in Sam's truck.

He drove out to the main fields where Sara and Annie grew most of their crops. Danté climbed out. He'd learned the first day there was no point in trying for conversation. There was nothing Danté had to say that Sam wanted to hear.

It was enough that he'd agreed to the terms of Danté's parole being served out on Turnabout rather than on the mainland. And one of the requirements was that he have a job. An honest one.

Before he could drive away, Sara waved him down. He heard her call out instructions to Danté who nodded and headed to the small building that held the equipment.

Then Sara jogged up to the passenger side of his truck. "Whoa. Nice shiner. I heard Winnie Haggerty was nearly on bended knee pleading you not to lock up the boys."

"They wouldn't press charges against each other,

and this—" he gestured "—just shows I don't move as fast as I used to. Vern was gunning for Teddy, not me."

"He always did have rotten aim." She folded her arms over the open window and leaned in a little farther. "I was starting to get worried when you and Danté didn't show up earlier. Everything okay?"

"Figured you'd be at your shop by now."

"Lily's working today. Handy to have plenty of quasi relations around to call on in a pinch. We're thinking about hiring her permanently. Otherwise she might have to move to the mainland. Just not enough jobs here."

He nodded. It was an ongoing problem. He looked beyond her for a moment, watching Danté reappear, a shovel propped up against his shoulder. He looked their way for a moment, then headed away between two tall rows. "I'll come back and pick him up at the usual time." It would mean a short day for Danté. But the old man's lateness had been Sam's fault.

Sara's eyes were thoughtful. "It wouldn't be a tragedy if you let him walk home the way everyone else does. He's not a two-year-old who has to be watched every minute."

"Yeah?" Seemed to Sam that whenever Danté *wasn't* watched, he couldn't keep himself from practicing his preferred profession. Con artist. Forger. Counterfeiter. They had all applied at one time or another. But even if Sam felt inclined to trust Danté, he was going to follow the parole terms to the letter. There wouldn't be any opportunity down the line for someone to accuse Sam of bending the rules.

Sara glanced over her shoulder at her fields. "Even you must admit it's a fine sight to see."

He ought to know the names of the plants, but he didn't. All he knew about the acres of green was that they were healthy. Growing. Some with brilliant flowers. Some without. Some days Annie and all of the kids from Castillo House were among the rows of plants. Bending, planting, plucking. But not today. Today it was Sara's usual handful of workers, Danté included.

"What? The sight of free labor?" Danté had accepted the job, but he categorically refused to allow Sara to pay him. Probably thinking that would put him on the good side of the law.

"The *smiles*, Sam." She gave him a sideways look. "Maybe you ought to be out there, too. See if a smile would cross your face. Working with the earth. There's nothing like it in the world."

"Thought you preferred to be in your workroom mixing and stirring up your lotions and goops."

She didn't take offense. "I do. But growing the stuff has its appeal, too. Where's the missus?"

Hot-footing it off the island as soon as she could. "She's—" Impossible. Beautiful. Hurting. Dangerous as hell to his own peace of mind. "Getting married to her business partner."

Sara's mouthed "oh" was either surprise at the announcement or surprise that he'd even shared the news at all. "I thought you and she were still married."

He pulled out his sunglasses and put them on. "We are."

"I see."

He doubted it. "I'll be back in a few hours."

"Leo has offered to come by, you know. Escort Danté home, since that's what you insist on." Her tone was diffident. Unusual for her. But she didn't seem surprised when he shook his head and she stepped back from the truck. "Sam? Seriously. Are you okay?"

He hadn't been okay for more than twenty-one months. "Yeah." Then because she was too nice for her own good, he summoned up a smile from somewhere. "Thanks for asking, though."

Her eyes were still searching. But after a moment she nodded and turned back to her fields.

He drove into town and unlocked the station. Took care of a handful of messages and went back out on a few calls. Wrote out a report for the town council's next meeting and generally tried not to keep looking at the clock.

But the day was crawling, and hanging around in his quiet office wasn't helping. He went over to the dining room at Maisy's Place and ordered a sandwich that he barely ate.

Delaney would be on the mainland by nightfall at the latest. She'd probably head straight to the airport to catch the first flight out. No staying over at a hotel to give herself some breathing room. That'd be for someone who didn't mind being still for ten minutes at a stretch.

Even on the flight, she'd pull out those files of hers. Immerse herself in the only thing she thought she was good at.

He finally left, assuring Maisy there was nothing wrong with the sandwich when she asked. He picked up

Danté and returned him to Etta's. The moment Danté
walked through the door, Sam knew the receiver would
note his old man's return, adding it to the log of his activities. Danté was allowed to leave the house only for
work. The monitor kept track of every one of his father's
comings and goings.

Once home again, Sam headed through his quiet
house. When he'd done the refurbishing, he'd found
some measure of peace in the fact that nothing there
reminded him of his time with Delaney. The house was
as different from her apartment as it could get. There
was no hint of her perfume that lingered in the air. None
of her clothes momentarily forgotten on the floor.

As he went out to the deck and threw himself down
on the chair, he didn't look at the ring box she'd left
sitting on the kitchen counter. He propped one foot on
the rail across from him and stared out at the gleam of
water on the horizon.

Almost directly below the deck rail, the water beat
against the rocky shoreline. The noise of wind meeting
ocean, ocean meeting rocks was constant. He was so
used to hearing it again, since he'd returned to Turnabout, that he hardly noticed it unless he deliberately
made himself hear.

Same way the sounds of the city had nearly disappeared into nothing when he'd lived there.

What had been vivid in his life then had been the job.
And then the woman.

His wife.

His gaze slid to the pile of clothing they'd discarded the day before. A heap of damp denim. Of thin black silk.

What they'd done was crazy and—once again—there was no one to blame but himself. Just like the first time—the night of her father's retirement party—the only thing driving him had been that unending need to be with her.

He leaned over and snatched up the white shirt he'd taken from her body. It was dry. No evidence remaining of the treatment it had received, except for the wrinkles.

The vision of what they'd done was too fresh. How long would it be before he could pass through the glass door from his bedroom without thinking of her? Without remembering how it had felt to sink into—

Hell.

He yanked his foot off the rail and threw aside the shirt. He didn't bother with the door as he charged out to his truck and drove down to Diego's. The ferry was still docked, but he could see the water churning around it. He hit the gas and drove down the center of the long dock, stopping next to the mooring.

He ignored Diego's yelling as he strode up the ramp and boarded the decrepit boat.

Delaney was already seated on one of the long benches, her hands folded over the top of the briefcase lying across her legs. As if she didn't want to touch any more of Diego's boat than necessary.

She stared at him as if he belonged in a padded cell. "What on earth is wrong with you?"

"No birth control pills."

"What?"

He approached her, not sure who he wanted to throttle more. Her. Or himself. "You came to the island with nothing but your briefcase."

The fine line of her jaw tightened. Her eyes were suddenly nervous. "So?"

"So, unless they got lost out on the road when you fell and the contents of your briefcase flew everywhere, you're not taking the pill."

"What'd you do? Look through every item I carry?" She rose, setting the briefcase behind her as if she were afraid he'd try to look through it again. "How *dare* you!"

"Pick up all the crap you were so bloody worried about when I thought you'd hurt your damned heel?"

She tilted her chin. "Maybe I did lose them that night."

"Delaney—"

"And maybe I didn't," she relented. "What does it matter? My birth control methods hardly concern you."

"After last night they damn well do concern me. We didn't use squat."

He saw realization slide into her eyes. She started to shake her head.

"You could be pregnant with my child."

Chapter 9

Delaney sat down. It was either that or fall down. Pregnant? "No," she countered harshly. "I'm not."

"Are you on the pill, then? Using some other invisible, undetectable means?"

She flushed, painfully aware of Diego Montoya stomping around Sam's truck on the dock, an outraged witness. "I told you, it's none of your business!"

"You're my *wife*." His voice lowered, but seemed all the more fierce because of it. "Are you using something or not?"

"Stop interrogating me!"

He started toward her, and she quickly rose, putting another row of benches between them.

"Not," she admitted tightly. "*I* wasn't sleeping with anyone."

He stopped cold. "You think I was?"

"Come on, Sam. You expect me to believe that you weren't?"

"You expect me to believe that *you* weren't and you're planning to marry the guy."

"But that's—"

"Different?" His voice was smooth. Silky. "How, exactly is it different, Dr. Vega? Oh, that's right. You went right back to using your maiden name as soon as I hit the door. You think because I'm a man it's different? Aren't you being *judgmental?*"

She exhaled slowly. Losing her temper would accomplish nothing. What would be the point of telling him that she hadn't gone back to using Townsend until she'd been in contact with Logan and Annie Drake regarding Alonso? "You're a very sexual man." She kept her voice factual and low, in deference to their audience of Diego.

"Spoken with all the dispassionate reasoning you're so fond of."

"You wanted to know what the basis of my opinion—"

"Save it." He shook his head and glared at her. "It doesn't matter, anyway. Until I know for certain that you're not going to pass off my child as someone else's, you're damn sure not leaving this island."

Shock turned her blood cold, and she forgot all about whether or not Diego could overhear them. "How can you think I'd do that?"

"How can you think I'd sleep with someone else when you and I are married?"

His voice seemed to echo in her head.

An impasse.

They were always at an impasse.

She opened her mouth, wishing for some inspiration, some words to bring reason to an unreasonable situation. But Sam was already walking away, the narrow ramp leading from the ferry to the dock vibrating under his boots. Her legs were unsteady and she sat down again, her gaze falling on the briefcase.

Her own fault. This was all her own fault. She could have lied to Sam. Told him she was using some other form of birth control. Or she could have just told him the truth. That her likelihood of ever conceiving again hovered somewhere between slim and none.

Either way, he couldn't make her stay on this island.

"Mrs. Sam?"

She looked up to see Diego standing nearby. He'd pulled off his grease-stained cap and was twisting it between his hands. "Yes?"

"I'm sorry, ma'am, but the sheriff, he doesn't want me to cross this afternoon."

"And you do what the sheriff asks, I suppose."

He shrugged apologetically and handed back the cash she'd used to pay the fare.

She took the money and slung the briefcase strap over her shoulder, disbelief joining her rioting emotions. She went down the ramp, her ridiculous shoes flip-flopping along the way. Sam waited on the precariously narrow space left by his truck, the passenger door open.

"I'm not pregnant," she snapped under her breath to him, "and you can't keep me a prisoner on this island. It's…it's *kidnapping* or something."

"Honey, I can do just about anything I want on this island."

"I'll file a complaint, then."

"Be my guest."

She narrowed her eyes. Bit the inside of her cheek to keep from screaming at him. From somewhere deep inside she found a reasonable tone. "Surely you can understand that I need to return to my practice. I have patients. I never intended to be here this long."

"Consider this a spontaneous vacation. Something you've never done in your entire life. When I know you're not pregnant, believe me, you can go with my blessing."

It was ridiculous that his words could still sting. "I'll take an early pregnancy test."

"You still need to wait a while before it's accurate."

"Dr. Hugo—that's his name, yes? He can do a blood test."

"Saves only a few days."

She pushed her briefcase into the truck and slammed the door shut. "Well, that's just dandy, Sam. When have you been doing all this research into the efficacy of pregnancy tests?"

His face hardened at her insinuation. "Dammit to hell, Delaney! I'm married to you. There hasn't been anyone *but* you since the first day I met you."

She pressed her shoulder against the side of the truck at that. "Oh, please. We knew each other for two years before we—"

His gaze didn't waver.

She swallowed a knot of uncertainty. Moistened her lips. Would she never understand him? "And—just for the sake of argument, mind you—what if I am pregnant?"

"You won't be filing those divorce papers again unless you want a custody fight on your hands."

Her stomach dropped out. "It wouldn't solve anything. We're still not—" she waved her hand after a moment, and heat rose in her neck "—compatible. For lack of a better word."

"Seemed pretty compatible out on my deck. And in my bed."

"I don't need you listing off each and every time we—"

"Made love?"

"—had sex." Her face heated when she realized Diego had come down the ramp and was listening avidly. She eyed him, and he hurried on, moving down the dock toward the weathered shack that housed what passed for an office.

Sam's lips twisted. "Call it whatever you want, Delaney. Doesn't change the facts. You can leave when we know one way or another."

Eons seemed to tick by, marked off by the rhythmic splash of water against the dock's pilings. Could she subject herself to a week or two in the same vicinity as Sam? Or should she just tell him the truth? "I have only one functioning ovary," she said baldly, going for the safety in truth no matter how private it was.

His brown eyes went black for a moment. "What?"

"You heard me."

"Since when?"

"What does it matter? The point is, it is unlikely at best that I would have conceived."

"Aside from your blood pressure that was too high because of the pregnancy, you were healthy as a horse before."

Look at all the evidence. That was a cop's motto.

She felt as if she'd jumped from the fat into the fire. "I had a, um, a tumor."

He stared at her. "Tumor," he finally repeated, as if the word tasted vile.

"It was benign," she said thickly. "And I'm fine." Physically maybe. "But I had to have a procedure, and my chances of ever becoming pregnant were considerably lessened."

"Procedure," his teeth closed on the word. "When?"

She hesitated for a moment. "Last winter."

"When you first tried mailing me back your wedding ring. Why didn't you say something before?"

"What for? The only reason I'm telling you now is because you're behaving so...so impossibly!"

He glared at her. Paced along the narrow edge of dock left by his truck. "Before. When you were having your *procedure*. Or I guess you didn't need me then, either. Probably had Do-Wright beside you, holding your hand."

She started. "Chad was speaking at a symposium in Canada."

"Then who was there with you?"

"Nobody."

The edge of his jaw was white. "Of course not. God forbid that Delaney Townsend should ever rely on someone else."

She rounded on him. "Oh, that's dandy, Sam. You're a fine one to talk about sharing a burden. Maybe we should talk about your father, since we're apparently unloading everything under the sun. Just what *is* it that Danté did that is so unbelievably unforgivable in your eyes? Because we both know that's something you've never been willing to discuss with me. Lord knows you couldn't possibly forgive someone for making a mistake, not when you're so perfect—"

"Shut up."

"No, I won't shut up." Her voice kept rising. She stepped closer to him. "You started this, Samson, with your insane mandate!"

"Thought you didn't believe in insanity."

She dragged in a breath, feeling as if her nerves were on fire, and there was nothing remotely pleasant about it. "Sometimes I really hate you."

"Yeah, well, get over it." His voice was cool again. "And get over the idea of leaving Turnabout."

People really did see red, she thought, as a haze of it seemed to settle over her vision. And there he stood. Tall. Intense. Immovable. Untouchable.

She took a step forward, planting her hands in the center of his chest.

And pushed.

He fell backward, his arms flying out. She had just enough time to be utterly and absolutely shocked at her own behavior before he hit and water shot upward in a high, wide splash.

She fell to her knees, closing her hands over the edge of the dock. He'd already come up to the surface. He gave his head a sharp shake, flicking his hair back. Treading water, he looked up at her.

She inwardly quailed. *Say something, Delaney. Use your wits.*

He swam to the ferry, grabbing onto a chain. Levered himself up until he found more substantial purchase. Heaved himself out of the water like some avenging movie hero.

He came back down the ramp. Stood over her, water sheeting off him, dampening her hands, her skirt where she still knelt.

His eyebrow lifted. "Feel better?"

She felt as insubstantial as a spent balloon hanging from a string. "I—I'm sorry."

"I could haul you in for that."

"I'm sorry!" She finally unfroze and scrambled to her feet. "You provoked me."

The pound of footsteps heralded Diego. "You okay, Sam?"

Sam's spiky-wet lashes didn't even glance away from her. "Fine, Diego. Go back to what you were doing."

She had an absurd desire to call the old man back when he muttered under his breath and scurried up the ramp. He returned a moment later carrying a vivid towel. He tossed it to Sam and scooted past them, heading back down the dock.

Judging by the wary look Diego had given her, she wouldn't have received help from that quarter even if she'd asked.

She watched Sam wipe his face, then sling the towel around his neck. He opened the passenger door of his truck again. His khaki shirt clung to every inch of his chest. Water dripped from his arm.

She slunk by and climbed up on the seat.

He shut the door with infinite care. Slamming it would have been less worrisome, she decided.

He went around the other side and got behind the wheel. Without a word to her, he competently backed down the length of the dock while she battered down visions of him accidentally driving off one side or the other.

When he'd wheeled around and was heading up the hill to the main road again, she finally spoke. "I don't want to stay with you."

"Now there's a news flash. But maybe you didn't notice well enough yet. Turnabout's not exactly overrun with lodging."

"It's Monday. Surely that inn—Maisy's—would have a room available by now."

He drove a little farther, then turned off and headed down a hill. He stopped in front of a building heavily surrounded by lush bushes and palm trees. Behind it, she could see several small cottages.

"Maisy's Place," he said. "Have at it."

She set her jaw and grabbed her briefcase. The bottom of it was damp from the water pooling around Sam on the seat. Without a word she climbed out of the truck and headed over to the inn, walked up the porch steps and went inside.

Ten minutes later she was trudging right back to the waiting truck. She climbed inside. The only person who'd been happy to see her had been little April Fielding, who'd given "Mrs. Sam" a big hug, while her grandmother was assuring Delaney that there was no room at the inn. "I suppose you knew Maisy's Place wouldn't have any vacancies."

"Yup."

She fell silent. Hating him all over again.

Only, her life would be a whole lot easier if she really did hate him.

She rested her elbow on the edge of the door where the window was rolled down, and covered her eyes with her hand.

What a tangled web she'd managed to make out of her life. All because she'd once again succumbed to Samson Vega.

"Stop sulking," he said as he put the truck in gear and drove away from Maisy's Place.

"I'm not sulking."

Mourning the past? Yes.

Sulking? No.

"Sounds convincing."

She looked sideways at him. "I'm not pregnant and I'm not staying on this island."

"We'll see."

When he parked in front of his house a short while later, she was the one who was shivering. She climbed out of the truck, hauling the briefcase she was seriously beginning to loathe with her, and followed him inside.

For the first time, he'd taken the truck keys with him.

As if she'd steal his truck?

He left a trail of water behind him as he walked inside and turned down the hall to his bedroom. She heard the soft snick of the door closing.

She exhaled, not entirely sure what she'd expected from him, but it wasn't this. She headed through to the kitchen and blindly shoved her briefcase onto the counter. It knocked to the floor the ring box she'd left sitting there before they'd left.

Muttering at herself for getting into this mess, she picked it up. Thumbed open the lid.

The small circle shone up at her. An unusual ring. Thin strands of gold in a delicate weave. And one she hadn't expected when he'd produced it the day of their wedding.

Elopement, she corrected.

Married in haste, repent even hastier.

She pushed away the thoughts. But that didn't stop her finger from prodding the ring from its position against the satin cushion.

The strands of woven gold felt warm, which was ridiculous. She poked, and the ring slid over the tip of her finger. She'd never worn it except on the day he gave it to her.

Had told him that it was too tight on her finger, thanks to the changes in her newly pregnant body.

She slipped it on.

It fit perfectly.

Her fingers curled closed.

What had he done with *his* wedding ring? When he'd produced hers at the ceremony, he'd also pushed a much larger, plain gold band into her hand to give back to him.

He'd worn it all the while they were together.

But he'd obviously stopped.

She heard his door again and hastily slid off the ring, tucking it back into its satin bed and shutting the lid. She was safely fumbling through her briefcase for her date book when he entered the kitchen.

His hair was still wet, but he wore dry jeans and a pale gray shirt open down the front. He didn't say a word, but she still felt a guilty flush warm her cheeks.

"You need to eat."

"I had lunch at Castillo House."

"You're too thin."

"So you've told me." His criticism stung. "That didn't seem to bother you too much last night. Or this morning."

"How do you think I know just exactly how thin you are?" He set an apple in front of her. "Start with that."

She considered throwing it at his head. Evidently part of the new not-so-nonviolent Delaney. "Yes, well, it's not going to happen again, that's for sure."

He'd pulled open the refrigerator and was rummaging inside. "You so sure about that?"

She made a face at his back. "Quite."

He closed the fridge and set a container on the counter, the corner of his mouth kicking up. As if he knew something she did not.

It annoyed her no end.

"Sex with you is not the end-all, be-all of existence, Samson."

He angled a look her way and his smile widened. Just a hair. One dangerous hair that wasn't mitigated at all by the very pedestrian way he was heating up a mug in the microwave. "Sounds like avoidance to me, Delaney." Above the bruise on his cheek, his eyes gleamed with biting amusement. "Wonder if Do-Wright would agree in this instance?"

"This has nothing to do with him."

"Kind of convoluted, aren't we? My wife is engaged to marry another man. So who should feel betrayed? Me for your engagement? Or him for you sleeping with your husband? Think we could make the rounds of the television talk shows with this scenario."

"I'm *not* engaged to him! How many times do I have to tell you that? I told him I couldn't marry him, okay? God, Sam. What will it take to satisfy you?" She snatched up the phone and brandished it. "Do you want to call him and check for yourself since you clearly don't trust *me?*"

His amusement dried, leaving him just looking dangerous.

The chime on the microwave pinged and he pulled out the mug, setting it, along with a spoon, in front of her next to the apple. "Trust wasn't my problem, Delaney. It was yours."

She winced. "Right. That's why you think you're going to keep me on this island until I *prove* there is no pregnancy."

He wasn't moved. "You'll stay of your own accord, Delaney. I know that much about you."

"I will not!"

"Yes, you will. Because some part of you has to wonder if the unlikely has happened. If you didn't, you'd already be gone. Do you want crackers with that?"

"You're as pigheaded as you ever were," she muttered.

He slammed a box of crackers on the counter, making her jump. "Yeah, well, baby, I love you, too," he said, teeth gritted, and strode out of the room.

Chapter 10

"Aren't you going to stop?"

Sam's foot eased off the gas as he watched Delaney walking farther ahead along the side of the road. A large plastic bag hung over her arm, bumping against her slender hip with each step.

"That is your wife I've been hearing about, isn't it?"

He slid a look Danté's way. "Hearing what?"

Danté's faint smile was wry. "This *is* Turnabout. One of the main occupations of the residents is gossip. Most folks are wondering if you're getting back together again."

"Then they can keep wondering."

"Even your grandma?"

Delaney had stopped walking for a moment. She bent

and shook something from her shoe, then resumed walking. If she was aware of his truck at this distance, she didn't show it. "If there's something to tell Etta, I will."

"You're not going to let her walk all the way out to your place. Hell, son, I raised you better than that."

Nothing could have set Sam's teeth on edge more. "You didn't raise me. Etta did." And because she had, he drove up beside Delaney.

She'd stopped and turned, lifting her arm to shade her eyes. She'd obviously been shopping. Sophie had a reasonable selection of clothes, but she didn't get too far into the designer stuff. Which accounted for the inexpensively simple sundress that was blowing against Delaney, outlining her long legs.

"Get in."

Her gaze went past Sam to his father sitting on the seat beside him, then back to Sam. "And if I don't want to?"

"Then walk." He heard Danté mutter under his breath at that.

She was considering it. Not that he blamed her, particularly. They hadn't spoken since the previous day. When he'd left the house early that morning, he'd left a note with his office number, just in case she wanted it. But he hadn't been surprised when she didn't use it. Too independent to need him for anything, and too angry to accept anything he might offer.

But she was also too polite to continue their war of wills in front of someone, and she finally walked around the truck.

Danté's smile was wide as he climbed out and held

the door. "Since my son isn't opening his mouth, I'll introduce myself. Danté Vega. And you're Delaney."

Sam caught the quick look Delaney shot him, then she was smiling herself, putting out her hand. But Danté, being Danté, couldn't just be satisfied with a handshake. Hell, no. He had to lift Delaney's hand in a courtly gesture, pressing his lips to the back of it.

"A lovely name for a lovely lady," he said. Then he helped her up in the front of the truck, and slid into the back despite her protests that she could sit there.

Danté had barely tugged the door closed when Sam put the truck in gear. His mood darkened as he listened to his father ask Delaney how she was enjoying her visit. What she thought of Turnabout. Had she been out to Luis's Point yet, where the views were particularly spectacular.

Putting an end to their chitchat took the upper hand, and he sped to Etta's. When he got there, he parked, wheels half on the grass. Then he climbed out himself, ensuring that Danté would get out on his side of the truck. He didn't want Delaney noticing the device that occasionally stuck out from beneath the leg of Danté's pants any sooner than necessary.

Preferably never.

But then Danté didn't head to the house. He stood there next to the truck, as if he had all the time in the world instead of only a few minutes before his absence from the house beyond the approved hour would be noted by the monitoring equipment. "You should come on in. Have some of Etta's lemonade. We'll talk."

"No," Sam answered flatly.

Delaney looked from him to his father, her eyes measuring. But she just directed a smile past Sam to Danté. "Another day, perhaps," she said. "It was very nice meeting you, Mr. Vega."

"Danté, girl. You're my daughter now, aren't you?"

Delaney seemed to pale a little, but she kept hold of her smile. "Danté."

He tipped an imaginary hat toward Delaney, then strode up the walk and through Etta's front door. Only when Sam was sure the man was inside the house did he drive away.

Staying well to her side of the bench seat, Delaney smoothed her hair back and held it in her hand to keep it from blowing. "Guess I know now what you would look like in twenty years."

He didn't reply. Whether she was pregnant or not, she'd be long gone before twenty years were up, and there was no point in pretending otherwise. "What'd you do out at Castillo House all afternoon?"

She angled a look his way. Whitecaps. Big ones. "Keeping track of my whereabouts? It's a wonder you even left me alone at all. Maybe you'd rather have handcuffed me to the bedpost to make sure I didn't escape when you're not looking."

"Handcuffs?" His lip kicked up. "Hmm."

She huffed. "Get over yourself."

"It's an island, Delaney. I got regular reports throughout the day from people who'd spotted my wife."

"From Mr. Montoya, too, I suppose. You've told him not to give me a ride to the mainland at all."

"No." Diego owned his own business; it was up to him who he catered to and didn't. It was merely convenient as far as Sam was concerned, that Diego—whose wife lived in San Diego because she loathed the inconvenience of living on the island—had his own well-earned feelings about where a wife belonged.

Old-fashioned, yes. Convenient for Sam? Definitely.

Delaney's lips were curved with disbelief. "Then why did he refuse to take me again when I went down there this morning? I was on time for the ferry run. Early, even. Of course, I had to walk the entire way considering that there was neither hide nor hair of you around your house this morning."

"Miss me?"

She sent him a withering look and settled her plastic bag on the seat more firmly. As if she needed that much more of a barrier between them than the stretch of seat. "I *can* try contacting a charter again."

"You could. But you haven't yet. Means you won't." He turned off the main road and headed up his crooked drive. "Did you eat?"

Her lips compressed. "I had a late lunch at Castillo House."

"Tutting over Alonso like a mother hen. Hasn't he worn out his welcome yet?"

"No," she said with exaggerated patience. "He's fitting in admirably. He spent nearly an hour talking my ear off. Of course he also slid in a warning or two about you."

"Right."

She let go of her hair to slide the thin white strap of her dress back up her shoulder. "Ironic, isn't it." Her hair blew from the open window, hiding her expression. "The way you both warn me against the other. You have *that* very much in common."

"Right." What he and Alonso had in common was Delaney. Period.

"Anyway, after lunch he went on his way. He's tutoring Caitlin in math so she'll be caught up with the senior class when school begins."

"What's he getting in return for that?"

"She's helping him with life sciences. She knows an incredible amount about nature. Birds in particular."

"That's it?"

"That's it."

He had a hard time envisioning that. The kid he'd known had never offered anything without getting something in return.

"You went shopping."

"Considering the one outfit I did bring shrunk in the rain? Yes, I went shopping."

"Good. Maisy's got a barbecue going tonight."

"Annie mentioned something about it."

"She's expecting me."

"Then go."

He looked at her.

"I don't want to go to a barbecue with you."

He shrugged and parked the truck in front of his house. "I'll call Maisy and tell her I'm staying in. With my wife." He climbed from the truck and closed the door.

Delaney's hand tightened around the plastic bag as she watched Sam head inside the house. What was worse? Attending a barbecue in public, or being alone with Sam?

Inside her head, her common sense was screaming the answer. For once, she decided to follow it.

She went inside. Found Sam heading out the rear door to throw out some seed for the birds. "When is it?"

"Whenever."

She counted to ten. "Is there time for me to clean up?"

His gaze roved over her, seeming to set off a flurry of nerves. "You look pretty clean to me. All that white? Practically...virginal."

She gave him a repressive look.

His mouth kicked up. "There's time. You got some shorts in that bag? A bathing suit?"

"Shorts." The only bathing suit Sophie had that fit her was a minuscule black bikini. Not likely.

"Wear 'em. We'll be on the beach."

"Any more orders?"

Amusement drifted into his eyes. "Not at the moment." Then he went out on the deck. She watched him throw out the seed and lean his arms on the rail as he watched the birds dive.

Another surreal moment. And realizing that she was staring, she quickly turned away.

While Sam had said she had time, it seemed all too soon before he was rapping on the bedroom door. "You about ready in there?"

She glanced at herself in the mirror, curtailing the urge to do something more with her hair. It was a beach barbecue, and she didn't want Sam thinking that she was going to any particular trouble with her appearance for *him*.

She snatched open the door. "Thought there was no hurry."

"There isn't." He leaned his shoulder against the doorjamb. Instead of the khaki uniform shirt and blue jeans, he wore an unbuttoned shirt and long cargo shorts that hung loosely around his hard hips.

Men half his age should look so good.

"Here." He held out his hand.

A key.

But he didn't lock his house.

"What's it for?"

"The golf cart. You didn't notice it beside the house when we drove up?"

All she'd been noticing was Sam. But she had no intention of admitting it.

"It's for you to use while you're here."

"Everybody pretty much walks on Turnabout." And her legs had gotten quite the workout that day as a result.

"Pretty much everybody lives closer to town, not a half-dozen miles out. But if you want to walk, suit yourself. These'll be more substantial than the flip-flops, though." He took his other hand from behind his back and handed her a shoebox.

"What is that?"

"Well, it ain't a snake." He wiggled the box.

She took it. Flipped off the lid to reveal pristine white tennis shoes. She lifted one out. Triple-A width. Narrow.

"Sophie didn't have these."

"I ordered them from a store in San Diego. Diego brought 'em by, along with the cart."

"Do you think this is going to get you on my good side?"

"God forbid. Last time we were on each other's good sides, we eloped to Vegas. Look how that turned out." His tone was dry as dust, and a bubble of laughter hit her unaware.

His smile was faint. "Let's go."

She exhaled a little, wondering how she was supposed to get through several more days when the next several minutes seemed a major challenge.

But he didn't head to his truck. He headed around the side of the house where a tidy little cart was indeed parked. But when she headed for the passenger side, he nudged her back toward the driver's side.

"Whoa, no. No. I don't want to drive."

"How long has it been?"

Months. Several. Like nearly two years' worth. "I haven't—"

She heard his breath escape. "Jesus, Delaney. You haven't driven since the accident, have you?"

She considered denying it. "No."

"Are you afraid?" There was nothing challenging or goading in his voice.

"Answering that would incriminate myself."

His expression was still. "You don't often drive, and two times in your life you've survived serious accidents."

"Yeah, well, third time might be a charm. Half this

island seems like it ends on a cliff." She wasn't entirely joking.

"And the road is well away from any drop-offs. Come on. Driving this little putt-putt is a good way to get back in the saddle. It hardly goes faster than you could ride a bike."

"And I haven't done that in even longer," she said.

He simply waited.

"The sun is going down. It'll be dark soon."

"We've got headlights. And I won't let you run into any potholes."

"This isn't a good idea."

"Get behind the wheel, Delaney. You'll be fine, and once you get over the hump, you'll be glad you did."

She exhaled noisily but capitulated. "Always giving the orders."

He pointed. "Key goes there."

"I know that," she huffed. Of course she hadn't. She'd never driven a golf cart in her life. She inserted the key.

"Forward. Reverse." He gestured. "Two speeds. Stop and go."

Her fingers flexed around the rigid rubber-covered steering wheel. It was considerably smaller than the one she remembered from her car.

"No time like the present," he prompted when they continued to sit there.

"Right." She turned the key. The motor hummed. The cart jerked and lurched when she hit the gas. It tipped wildly when she turned too sharply.

If he laughed at her, she'd kick him. "This isn't at *all* like driving a car."

"Pretend you're at an amusement park in the play motor cars," he suggested. "Imagine there are rails holding you safely to the center of the road."

"I wish." She pressed the gas too hard again, and the thing shot up over the crest of the road. Sam's hand smoothly grabbed the steering wheel, and the cart straightened out. "You should drive."

"And miss out on a premium-ticket ride like this?" He shook his head. "Nothing doing." His hand left the steering wheel. "Road curves slightly to the right up ahead."

"I see it." The last vestiges of the setting sun provided a warm, red glow across the road. She followed the curve without mishap. The cart buzzed along, Sam pointing out spots to avoid, just as he'd promised.

They weren't traveling at the speed of light—nor the speed of Sam's heavy-duty vehicle—but it was quick enough. Once she felt more comfortable at handling the thing, she let herself look beyond the road directly ahead.

And her foot lifted off the gas as her gaze was caught by the sight of the sunset. The golf cart inched along and drifted to a gentle stop.

"Good sunset tonight," he said.

Good? The sky seemed to drip with every color of the spectrum, and every color reflected back up off the ocean. It was so vivid it was like walking into a painting. "It's magnificent." She'd never seen anything like it.

"Wait until you see the sky when the stars come out. Makes you feel like a tiny speck in the scheme of things, but at the same time feel like you're woven into the fabric of it all. It's kind of addictive."

She couldn't even summon a tart comment about Sam waxing philosophical.

She looked up and found his gaze on her. Not the sunset.

Addictive, indeed.

She quickly pushed the gas pedal, and the cart shot down the road. At least she'd forgotten to be nervous about driving. Some part of her mind wondered if he'd done it deliberately for that very purpose.

Sam pointed out another curve, and they headed down a hill that took them right onto the powdery white sand where a fire burned brightly in a pit. Music was playing from somewhere.

"Leave the key," he advised when he stepped away from the cart. "Safer than chancing losing it in the sand."

She slid off the seat, tugging at the hem of her shorts and wishing they were longer. There seemed to be just as many people on the narrow beach as there were at Castillo House the night she'd arrived.

Sam grabbed her hand, pulling her after him.

She hurriedly slid out of the sandals before she fell flat on her face at his brisk pace. She didn't know where he was heading, but was glad that he stopped periodically to greet various clusters of people. Delaney saw Maisy Fielding standing close to the fire, tending the meat that sizzled on the grate. She also saw Etta and Janie. Even young April Fielding. She didn't see Danté.

Within minutes her calves burned, and the soles of

her feet were tender. So much for kickboxing and the treadmill at her gym. Walking barefoot over shifting sand was a workout all on its own.

Sam's strong, well-shaped legs had no problem dealing with the exertion, she noticed.

"Sam." She finally tugged back on his hand, resisting his forward momentum. "Slow down before I get a Charlie horse."

He stopped. "Sorry."

She looked around them as she lifted one leg, then the other, trying to stretch out the knots in her calves. Though she'd feared drawing undue attention—she certainly had when she'd walked to town that morning—nobody seemed overly curious now. "Is the entire population of Turnabout down here?"

"Probably half. Maisy does a barbecue like this a few times every summer. Lot of people. Lot of food. Lot of drink."

Delaney straightened. "Are you here as a guest or to keep the peace?"

"On this rock? I'm never off duty. Come on. The food won't last forever with this group."

She realized there were several long tables set up in the curve of the seawall. She hadn't noticed them earlier because of the people milling about. "I ate a late lunch, remember?"

"Right. With Alonso."

Her chin lifted. "And Dr. Weathers and the rest of the children there." It had been noisy and chaotic and quite...wonderful.

"Suit yourself." He continued over to the tables, though. Loaded up a plate and grabbed a can of soda from an ice-filled barrel. Then, without paying her any heed, he joined the group closest to the fire.

The bodies moved, seeming to part and allow him entrance. Sara was part of the group.

Delaney turned away. She saw Caitlin sitting in a lawn chair down by the water's edge and headed that way. "How'd the tutoring go?"

Caitlin shrugged. "Fine. Don't know what good it'll do, though." Her hand smoothed over her protruding belly. "Can't see going back to school at all, much less while looking like a beached whale."

"Sure you can. Got to finish so you can go on to study ornithology, right?"

Caitlin just shrugged. She rubbed her hand over her belly again. "Have you ever had a baby?"

Delaney tried not to wince. She shook her head. "Do you know if it's a boy or a girl?"

"It's a boy. Dr. Weathers suggested that I start picking out names or something. Like it'd be fun." Her lips twisted a little.

"Did you?"

"Zachary. Zach. It was my dad's name." She fingered the hem of her billowing maternity shirt. "He was in the Navy. Died a long time ago on some secret operation. But he knew Logan, I guess."

"That's how you came to live at Castillo House." Annie had mentioned it. In fact, a lot of the children there seemed to have some sort of connection to Logan.

She knew he'd traveled widely, which perhaps explained the diversity among his and Annie's charges.

Delaney glanced over to the fire pit. Sam actually had a smile on his face.

"Yeah. Logan heard about the fire." Caitlin's expression was sad. "That's how they all died. In a fire. Only reason I wasn't there was 'cause I'd snuck out to meet my—" her voice cut off. She looked beyond Delaney. "Hi, Teddy. Um. This is—"

"Delaney," she filled in, smiling at the gangly young man.

"Teddy Haggerty," he returned, but his eyes were all for Caitlin. "Here." He held out a bottle of soda to the girl. "I brought you something to drink."

Delaney pushed to her feet. "Think a drink sounds good, myself."

"Oh." Teddy smiled awkwardly. "I can—"

"No, no. I'll get it myself." She smiled at Caitlin and headed back toward the fire pit, veering only long enough to shove her hand into the icy barrel and extract a can of her own.

Sam had demanded her presence on the island?

He'd get it.

She slid into the group, taking a spot across the fire pit from him and Sara, and smiled brightly when his gaze found hers. She popped open her can and lifted it in a silent toast.

Even in the red-and-orange dance of firelight, she could see the disapproval in his expression, and she realized that her blind grab from the barrel had secured her a can of beer.

Drink the alcohol. Don't drink the alcohol. That was the question. If she did, he'd consider it foolhardy. If she didn't, she'd be admitting the possibility that he was right. She could be pregnant.

His focus on her was palpable. As real as the reggae music underscored by the murmur of the ocean. As real as the orange sparks dancing off the flames in the fire pit, as the thick bulge of sand pushing up against the soles of her feet and squishing between her toes.

Pregnancy isn't entirely impossible.

She wanted to ignore the little voice inside her head. But she'd learned long ago that wanting and getting were two distinctively different things.

So she acquiesced to the little voice and exchanged her beer for a sensible bottle of water.

If anything, Sam's expression seemed to sharpen when she did so. Or maybe it was her imagination. A trick of the firelight.

Whatever it was, she felt as if it was burning through the layers of the past, leaving it in ashes.

She couldn't tear herself from the web of Sam's gaze.

What if she was pregnant?

Chapter 11

"Doc!" Alonso jogged over to her. "I've been calling you for five minutes. Come on. We're playing volleyball."

She finally dragged her gaze from Sam's. Alonso was very nearly grinning, and the knot in her nerves loosened a little. "I haven't played volleyball in years."

"So?" He dropped his arm over her shoulder and urged her along the sand. "You can be on the other team."

She laughed, feeling a little light-headed. "Gee. Thanks."

Logan, Dr. Weathers and two girls—ten-year-olds, Mary and Eileen, whom she'd met that afternoon—were on one side of the net. On the other side, Annie held the white ball as she pointed out positions to the three young boys on her team. There was also a tall, good-looking man Delaney didn't recognize.

"Come on, Delaney." Annie waved her over. "We've got 'em running."

"In your dreams, Annie," Logan assured. Alonso trotted over to Logan's side, bending over to hear something Mary said. He nodded, high-fived her and took his spot in the sand.

Sam hadn't left the fireside, but he was definitely watching them. She'd ignore him. That was all.

Right.

She pushed the bottom of her water bottle in the sand alongside several others and joined Annie's team. The net had been set up close to the water where the sand was more firmly packed.

"You've met Sam's brother, right?" Annie tossed the ball to the man.

Delaney started. Of course. The resemblance was there. But his looks lacked the hard edge that Sam possessed. "Leo?" She smiled awkwardly at the man.

Leo seemed to feel no such awkwardness. His smile was easy and appealing. "The good-looking brother," he said. "Glad Sam didn't scare you off before we met."

"Come on, folks," Logan called out. "Get the ball moving."

"Impatient, aren't you," Annie retorted.

"Yeah." Logan smiled at his wife.

The younger kids giggled, Logan's innuendo thankfully slipping over their heads. Leo served the ball and the game was on.

It was hardly a graceful one. But it was fun and by the time Alonso lifted Mary up on his shoulder to spike the ball over the net for the winning point, Delaney was laughing harder than she had in months.

Twenty-one, at least.

She stumbled over to her water bottle and collapsed on the sand, her side aching. She wasn't the only one who collapsed. Annie plopped down beside her, returning Logan's and Alonso's gloating comments with dizzying speed.

Leo headed to the food and drink, and Dr. Weathers headed off by herself. "She gave us her resignation letter just before we left for the barbecue," Annie confided quietly. "I was so happy when she agreed to come here, but not everyone takes to living so far from conveniences."

"No golden arches," Logan agreed as he threw himself down beside Annie, looping his fingers through hers. "Only a few shops. Living on Turnabout isn't for everybody."

Delaney stared after the psychologist. One great plus of Castillo House was not only Annie and Logan's dedication, but the quality of their staff. "What are you going to do?"

Annie smiled faintly. "Don't suppose you want a job, do you?" Just as quickly she waved her hand, barely giving her question a chance to settle in Delaney's mind. "I know. You're way overqualified. Don't mind me. I'm just feeling a little…panicked."

"Don't worry so much," Logan told her. "We'll find a replacement. Things have a way of working out."

"As we know," Annie's face lightened, and she leaned against Logan for a moment.

The look the Drakes exchanged was so full that Delaney felt intrusive. She turned her gaze toward Alonso, still by the volleyball net. The younger girls and boys were on one side, he on the other.

"He's good with the children," Annie commented after a moment.

"Yes." It gave her hope. Delaney watched him lob the ball over the net to the younger kids. Again and again. He didn't break a smile. Not quite. But she had no question that he was enjoying himself.

It was what she'd wanted most for him. A life not shadowed by his father's activities or his mother's death. A life he could call his own, ruled by decisions of his own making. Decisions that he could respect.

"Here. Looks like you could use a new one."

She realized Leo was standing over her, holding out a fresh bottle of water. Hers was empty. "Thank you." She reached up for it and tried not to be obvious when she looked for Sam. He was still near the fire pit.

With Sara.

Leo sat down beside her. "Quite a surprise. Learning Sam was secretly married."

Delaney busied herself opening the water. It hadn't been a secret from everyone. Only *his* family. *His* friends.

He'd once accused her of being ashamed of him, but it would seem the truth was the other way around. And it hurt.

"He never did like advertising his mistakes."

She stiffened.

"Leo!" Annie swatted him. "What a thing to say."

"Hey. I didn't mean that the way it sounded." He looked back at Delaney. "I didn't. I just meant that if he hadn't blown it with you, we'd have met you before now."

"I don't think you're improving the situation, man," Logan said dryly. He pulled Annie to her feet. "Let's see if there's any of my aunt's ribs left."

Leo grimaced when they were gone. "I didn't mean to offend you. Seriously."

"All right." She looked again past him. Logan had stopped next to Sam, talking. "Maisy is Logan's aunt?"

"Not technically." He leaned back on his elbows, his long legs stretched straight out, bare feet crossed casually at the ankles. He was more slender than Sam. "Logan's mother was a cousin of Henry—Maisy's husband. Drakes and Fieldings and Vegas go way back."

"One big happy family," Delaney murmured.

Leo's crooked smile was wry. "On the good days. On the bad?" He shook his head. "Not so much. Sam doesn't talk about what happened in New York."

The comment came out of the blue. Obviously there was more to Leo than there appeared. "He certainly didn't talk about me," Delaney agreed.

"With his job. Why he was fired."

She stopped watching Sam at that and looked at Sam's brother. "Fired?" He'd never told her. She'd assumed he'd quit because he'd been that determined to get away from *her*. Otherwise, surely he'd have stayed and fought the ridiculous claim that he'd stolen evidence from a case. She wondered if her father knew, but dismissed it. If he had, he'd have probably told her. Another mark against her in a near lifetime of them.

"If he'd had any other place who'd hire him, he'd have gone there rather than come back here," Leo assured.

She cast a look Sam's way again. He was still talking with Logan. Annie's and Sara's heads were close together. Delaney knew the two women were business partners and very good friends. Then Sara threw back her head, her musical laughter ringing out.

"She's very beautiful."

"Yeah."

Something in Leo's tone caught her, and she glanced at him. "Are you and Sara…?"

His lips twisted, and for a moment he looked remarkably like Sam. "Not anymore."

Then a young woman with fire-engine-red hair, wearing a bikini top and brief shorts strolled by. She smiled at Leo as she passed and he sat forward, his expression clearing as if the frown had never been. "Gotta go," he said. "Duty calls."

Amused, Delaney watched him catch up to the redhead.

Sam walked up beside her, also watching Leo.

"Who is she?"

Sam shrugged. "A visitor. Never seen her before. That won't stop my brother, though. Believe me. He takes after Danté. Follows trouble wherever he can."

"Really? Your brother seemed quite nice, to me." Sitting on the wet sand while Sam towered over her put her at a severe disadvantage. But standing would prove it, so she remained right where she was. "And your father was charming earlier today. The only thing *he* was following was your pointed glare that he go inside the house."

"Yeah, he's charming all right," Sam agreed. "But don't let him fool you. Danté takes the shortest route to getting what he wants."

"Some might consider that an admirable trait. Efficient, if you will." For about the millionth time, she wished she knew what had caused the dissension between Sam and his father.

"And how often have you applied the shortest route to getting what you want out of life?"

"Knowing how you feel about your father, I half expected him to be some sort of ogre."

"Yeah, well, don't get too smitten."

"With whom? Your father, or your brother?"

"Either. I told you. Leo's like Danté. His eye roves as steadily as the tide comes in and goes back out."

"Are you certain?" Regardless of the redhead, she'd seen the way his brother had responded to Sara. "Maybe you don't know him as well as you think you do."

"And you do after a game of volleyball and a chat in the sand?"

"Objectivity, Sam. Sometimes it's easier to see what's right in front of your face." She met his gaze steadily. Then sighed. She pushed to her feet and brushed the sand from the seat of her too-short shorts. "And we both know that I never learned how to take the easy route in my life. You're proof of that." She hesitated for a moment, wishing he'd say something, but he didn't.

She turned away. She made it several feet.

"Laney."

Something curled through her, something painful, something sweet. She stopped and looked back at him. "Yes?"

His jaw cocked. The breeze lifted his loosened shirt away from his chest and pushed his dark hair over his forehead. His fingers propped on his hips.

Say what it is you have to say, Sam. She wanted to yell the words even as she wanted to deny them. Because he'd either break her heart all over again or he wouldn't.

Instead, a lifetime of reticence held her tongue, and she could only stand there wishing for something she'd never been able to voice.

Eons seemed to pass before Sam took one step toward her.

Her heart climbed into her throat.

And a short, sharp scream rent the air.

Delaney nearly jumped out of her skin as she turned to look toward the sound. "What on earth?"

Sam was already running across the sand.

She followed him, neither as adept nor as fast at running on the shifting sand. By the time she caught up, a crowd had formed. A crowd she couldn't see over or around.

But when she heard Alonso's raised voice, she didn't care. She pushed her way through only to find Sam and Alonso squared off over Mary who lay hunched on the ground, holding her leg.

She knelt next to the girl, dismay sweeping through her. "What happened? Where're Annie and Logan?"

She gently brushed a tangle of hair away from the girl's face. "You hurt your leg?"

"'Lonso was—"

"He dropped her," Sam said flatly.

"It was an accident!" Alonso looked braced.

Annie raced up and dropped to her knees beside Delaney. "Logan's getting Dr. Hugo," she said breathlessly. Her face looked strained, but her touch was gentle on Mary. "He'll get you fixed up in no time."

The girl buried her face in Annie's lap, crying. "It hurts."

"I know, sweetheart." Annie leaned over the girl, comforting her as much as she could.

"I didn't mean to hurt her," Alonso said roughly. Then he turned and pushed through the people circled around them.

Delaney scrambled to her feet, hastily shoving them back into her sandals as she cast a look Sam's way. "We have to go after him. It *was* an accident, Sam."

She realized she was holding her breath, waiting for him to agree.

He didn't.

She exhaled, her disappointment heavy. She stepped up to him, her voice low. "Must be dandy to be so secure in your beliefs. Everything nice and tidy in the columns of wrong and right. He's a *boy*. Even when he had parents, he wasn't given the benefit of proper guidance. Maybe he's gotten into some trouble in the past, but he hasn't done anything new for a long while now. Is your childhood so pristine that you can really look down your nose and judge everyone around you and write off those who don't meet your standards?"

She realized she was waiting for an answer that would never come from him. She turned on her heel and followed the direction Alonso had taken.

She walked up toward the edge of the beach where the golf carts and bicycles and a few vehicles were parked.

There was no sight of Alonso's lanky form.

Despite her words to Sam, Delaney couldn't help the fear that ran through her. It was an island. Alonso couldn't go far. But he knew there was one sure way to get *off* the island. All it would take would be one call from the local authorities—Sam—and there'd be nothing more Delaney could do for the boy.

She bit the inside of her lip, her eyes scanning. Along the narrow stretch of beach that was fairly empty since most of the folks were still surrounding Mary, the fire pit and the food tables. She could hear no scrape of size-eleven tennis shoes on the gravel. No shadows moving amongst the assortment of carts.

"Alonso!"

"You think yelling his name is gonna work?" Sam came up behind her.

She rounded on him, her emotions bubbling out of control. "You bloody selfish bastard." She shoved at his chest. "This is *your* fault."

"Hold on." He grabbed her hands. "He can't go far. It's an island, for Christ's sake."

"An island where he's certain you don't want him." She yanked away, raking her hands through her hair.

Then she heard it. The sound of an engine turning over.

She looked around, barely aware of Sam doing the

same thing, and saw a small pickup shoot out from the motley collection of vehicles. In the moonlight she caught the slant of Alonso's face, the glint of the gold earring he wore. Her stomach dropped to her toes.

"I see he still has hot-wiring vehicles on his list of skills." Sam grabbed her arm and practically dragged her over to their golf cart. He got behind the wheel and flicked the key. "Hurry up," he snapped.

Delaney got in. "He might have used a key, you know," she huffed pointedly, "considering how everyone leaves keys in ignitions around here."

He floored it, and the cart sped over the sand.

"He's going on the road!" Delaney craned her head to watch the progress of the truck while Sam headed down the beach, barely seeming to wait for people to jump out of his way.

"So will we," Sam assured. He veered around the people circling Mary. Delaney caught a glimpse of Logan and Dr. Hugo as they passed.

"This is your fault," Delaney said again. "All Alonso wants is to be accepted. To please you."

"To please *you*," Sam corrected. Wind blew through the open cart. He turned the wheel, and sand spun from the tires as he headed up a narrow walking path. The motor whined, laboring. Then they reached the crest and came out on the road, considerably farther down.

"Shortcuts," he said as he stopped. "They're all over the island if you know where to look. Get out of the cart."

"No."

"What do you think I'm going to do to him? Beat him up? You said it yourself. He's a kid."

"No."

"Come on, Delaney. He's pissed at me. I don't want you getting between us. Last time, he was only twelve when he went for my throat."

"All he did was try to punch you."

"And you were in the way. Between us."

As usual.

Delaney stayed in her seat. "I'm not getting out."

He glared at her. She glared back.

A war of will.

He swore and hit the gas again. Delaney looked away, swallowing. She'd fully expected him to bodily eject her from the cart.

"That's Annie's truck he stole," Sam said as they buzzed along the road. "Not exactly the way to keep himself in her and Logan's good graces."

"He's convinced you're going to get him off the island, anyway. Maybe he's right."

"You'd try the patience of a saint."

Her eyes stung. She blinked rapidly. "We're not going to catch up to him in a golf cart."

"Yeah, but he's going to come to the end of the road."

"You told me years ago that Turnabout was a sleepy, boring little place."

"It used to be," he muttered. He veered suddenly, and the cart fishtailed to a stop.

Then Delaney saw Annie's truck.

Crumpled against the corner of a brick building. A sign hung over it. Island Botanica.

Alonso had hit Annie and Sara Drake's shop.

"God." She jumped out of the cart, nearly falling on her face when her sandal caught in a crevice in the pavement. Sam caught her, lifting her along with him as he ran to the truck.

He yanked open the passenger door. The interior light came on. The airbag had deployed, and it hung limply from the steering wheel. A thin cloud of powder still danced in the air, settling weightlessly on the seat.

Delaney covered her mouth, looking from the empty interior to the area around the truck. "Where is he?" Her voice sounded as panicked as she felt.

"There." Sam gestured.

Alonso sat on the curb across the street, some distance down the road, nearly hidden by the sign advertising the sales at Sophie's store.

She ran over to him, her sandals flapping. "Have you *lost* your mind?" She couldn't believe that particular statement came out of her mouth. She crouched down in front of Alonso, her hands running over his arms, his legs. "Are you okay?"

He brushed off her touch. "Leave me alone."

Hurt congealed inside her. But she and Alonso had been through too many times together; they hadn't always been pleasant. She caught his chin in her hand, looking into his face. Her brother had drunk and gambled and thrown away his life on a dozen other minor, yet illegal, activities. She'd be damned if she'd stand back and watch Alonso take the same path. "Are you hurt?"

He looked away, making a face. "No."

Fear dribbled out of her, leaving her weak. She leaned forward and kissed his forehead. "Idiot," she murmured.

But Alonso didn't want her fawning over him any more than he ever did. He leaned away, giving Sam a sideways look. "So you gonna arrest me, finally?" Even though he still sat on the curb, looking up at them, his words were full of challenge. "You've been wanting to since I was eleven years old and—"

"Nobody's getting arrested, Alonso," Delaney said hurriedly. She looked up at Sam. "Right?"

His face was hard, his expression uncompromising. "What happened with Mary?"

"What do you think? I threw her on the ground."

"Alonso!"

"Well?" He pushed to his feet. "Do you think he's gonna believe anything I have to say? He never did before."

"And half the time you couldn't tell the truth from a hole in the ground," Sam said flatly. *"What happened with Mary?"*

Delaney caught Alonso's hand. He shook her off.

He stomped off several feet away from them. Stopped. Stomped back. His head cocked, attitude reeking from him in a tangible wave. "I was giving her a ride on my shoulders," he finally said, his voice stiff. He looked at Delaney rather than Sam. "She wanted to stand. I told her no but she tried anyway, and before I knew it, she fell. It was an *accident.*"

Then he turned his back on them both, his hands on his hips as he surveyed the wreckage of Annie's truck.

"Doesn't matter," he muttered. "They're gonna ship me back with you anyway, V."

"Is that why you did it?" Sam's voice was hard. "Because you want to go back to New York? Back to wearing an ankle bracelet where you can't leave your house unless your probation officer tells you that you can? Or maybe you want to hook up with your old pals. The ones who are doing five-to-seven in—"

"Shut up. Get out your cuffs if you even need 'em in this hole of a place." Alonso's voice was thick.

Delaney saw him swipe his thumb over his eye. She felt like crying herself. She folded her hands together. Sam stood to one side, his stance unrelenting. Alonso stood to the other side of her, his stance defensive.

Too familiar, she thought. Way too familiar.

"A few nights in a cell would do you some good," Sam said after a moment.

Delaney closed her eyes, dismay sweeping through her.

"And maybe you'll still have that chance," he went on. "If Annie presses charges for taking her truck and wrecking it."

Her eyes snapped open as she stared at Sam, hardly able to believe her ears. A reprieve?

"Like that's *not* gonna happen," Alonso said under his breath.

"You didn't just wreck the truck," Sam continued.

"You hit the side of her business. You couldn't have been more stupid if you'd tried."

Alonso bristled. Delaney wrapped her fingers around his arm. She felt his muscle flex, but he didn't shake her off. "We'll go back," she said quickly. "And we'll talk to Annie and Logan. You'll apologize. You'll offer to pay off the damage."

"You mean *you'll* pay off the damage."

Delaney looked to Sam. "What's that supposed to mean?"

"You bought his way into Castillo House in the first place, didn't you?"

Secrets have a way of coming out. "If I did or didn't, it hardly concerns you."

Beside her, Alonso swore, and then he did shake off her hand. "Man, I don't need your money."

Sam snorted. "Kid, all you've got going for you is Delaney's money."

She stomped her foot. Hard. Dust puffed up from the street. "Stop it. Right now."

They both looked at her, Alonso showing his surprise only slightly more obviously than Sam did.

"This is just a setback," she told Alonso. "And it's not an unforgivable one, as long as you're actually sorry that it happened." She looked up into his face. "Well? Come on, Alonso. If you're sorry, you've got to say the words!"

His lips twisted. "I didn't mean to hurt Mary."

She steeled herself against softening. "I know you didn't. But now you're going to face up to what you *did* do. Agreed?"

His gaze slid to the side. He lifted one shoulder. She knew from experience that it was as much of an assent as she was going to get.

Then she looked at Sam. "Okay?"

He lifted his shoulder, too. Eerily similar to Alonso's movement. But all he said was, "For now."

In other words, the reprieve was probably temporary. But she would take what she could get.

Chapter 12

Mary's leg was not broken. Dr. Hugo's X-ray had confirmed the injury was only a sprain.

When Delaney went to Castillo House the next day to visit, Mary was hobbling around on a pair of miniature crutches, soaking up the extra attention she was receiving like a thirsty little sponge.

Alonso, however, was refusing to interact with everyone, including Dr. Weathers, Logan and even Mary. He'd apologized to all of them the night before, and promised to work off what it cost to make repairs to the truck and the building. Logan and Annie had agreed with more alacrity than Delaney might have expected.

"He's out by the basketball hoop," Annie told her. "He worked in the fields this morning from dawn on," she added, recognizing the worried sound Delaney made. She smiled a little. "When Logan was a teenager, he ran a truck into the side of Maisy's Place. These things can happen to anyone."

"Thanks, Annie."

Alonso was right where Annie had said he would be. Bouncing the ball, occasionally shooting it straight through the basketball hoop. Mostly just looking very much alone.

"School will be starting in about a month," she greeted as she walked closer. "The school has a basketball team. They make trips across to San Diego to compete with the schools there."

"Ain't gonna be here, anyway." He didn't look at her as he shot another basket and jogged forward to rebound his own ball. His movements were loose-limbed and easy. The gym teacher at his last school had bemoaned losing Alonso's natural athleticism. "Your cop'll make sure of that."

"Sam isn't my *cop*."

"Your husband, then," he countered.

"Come on, Alonso. You've already given Sam a reason, and he didn't take the opportunity." She darted forward and stole the ball—successful only because he hadn't expected it. "You like it at Castillo House, don't you? You were having fun with the children last night until Mary fell. And she's going to be okay." She bounced the ball a few times. Shot it at the basket. It bounced off the backboard, and Alonso caught it.

"Man, you can't shoot for sh— squat." He dribbled the ball around her. Sank a basket. Showing off.

"So I'll try again." She held up her hand, waiting for him to toss the ball to her. He did, with a bounce. The ball hit her in the stomach before she managed to catch it. There hadn't been any phys-ed teacher who'd moaned *her* loss back in school.

She'd been brainy and shy. Not fitting in well with either the rich kids or the poor.

She bounced the ball a few times, enjoying the hollow thwack as it hit the cement. She eyed the basket, but was far more focused on Alonso.

"The cop's never gonna let me live here for good."

She lifted the ball in a bad imitation of the way he'd thrown it. She missed the basket. "And you want to?"

"What do I care? Used to getting passed around." He passed her the ball again.

"I think you do care. Is the food here bad?"

He eyed her. Shook his head.

"Mattress lumpy?" At the halfway house, he'd had to sleep on a thin cot. "The children too loud that you can't read at night?" She kept him in a steady supply of fantasy novels though he denied enjoying them. She took another shot. A little more determined. The ball completely missed the backboard.

"No. But it doesn't matter," Alonso said. "He doesn't want me here."

He retrieved the ball and jogged over to her. The ball rolled off his palm into hers.

"Lift it like this."

She copied his gesture. He stepped behind her, adjusted her hands. "Aim for the corner of the box."

She did. The ball bounced off the backboard. It circled the rim. Once. Twice. Teetered. Dropped through the net.

Delaney was surprised at the glee that danced through her. She grinned up at Alonso and caught his hands, squeezing. "Things will work out."

"And you're still gonna leave. Only reason you haven't already is 'cause of *him*." He tugged his hands free, scooped up the ball and sank another basket.

Delaney pushed her hands in the side pockets of the skirt she wore. "Surprisingly enough, I'll miss you, too, kiddo. But you can call me whenever you want, Alonso. We'll still talk. I've told you that."

He cast her a long look. "Yeah. Whatever." He tucked the ball under his arm. "I'm going inside."

Delaney sighed. After a long while she followed. He'd closed himself in his room. He didn't respond when she knocked.

She refused Annie's invitation to lunch and drove to town in the golf cart. Principles forced her to stop off at Maisy's Place to see if there was an available room or cottage yet.

There wasn't.

She left the inn, not sure if she was relieved or disappointed, and drove up the hill. At the sight of The Store, she stopped. Thirty minutes later, she came back out with a bag of groceries, another new sundress and a package of undershirts.

Sam's truck was parked in front of his office when

she drove past. The urge to stop and see him hit with considerable force. She even lifted her foot off the gas pedal of the little cart, coasting to a stop.

And what would she say to him if she went inside?

Then the closed blinds on the door swung, and a moment later the door opened. She caught her breath, then expelled it in a weak stream at the sight of Henrietta Vega coming out.

The elderly woman noticed Delaney loitering in the golf cart and waved, thumping her way across the sidewalk. "Talk some sense into him," she greeted unceremoniously.

"About what?" Delaney asked cautiously. She wasn't sure what intimidated her more. Approaching Sam after the way things had ended the night before, or talking with his iron-haired grandmother. The corona of gray hair twined around her head reminded Delaney of a crown, and goodness knows the woman demanded attention in a royal way.

"Ignoring his family, of course," Etta snapped. "And I won't have it. Now that we're all here again, I just—" thump "—won't have it." Thump, thump.

Still, Delaney hesitated. "Mrs. Vega, *Etta,*" she corrected hurriedly at the look she received, "I think you should be working this out with Sam."

"You think I haven't tried that?" Etta's eyes snapped. "A more stubborn man doesn't exist than my grandson. He wants something, he doesn't stop until he gets it. And the opposite is just as true. You ought to know that better than anyone."

Delaney's cheeks warmed. "What is it that you want Sam to do?" She far preferred Etta's focus to be on Sam than on *her.*

"Come to dinner next Sunday. He's missed once, and that's too much." Exaggerated patience filled the woman's voice. "Tell him you want to be there. He'll bring you."

"But I...Etta, Sam and I aren't, well—"

"What?" Etta waved her cane. "Speak up, girl. Can't abide hemming and hawing about. You gave me the impression the other day that you had some spine."

"Etta." Sam came out of his office. He didn't look at Delaney. Nothing new. He hadn't really looked at her since he'd left her and Alonso to deal with Logan and Annie over Mary and the truck. "Leave it alone."

Etta's voice abruptly went fragile. "Samson, I'm an old woman. You don't know how many more Sundays I have left in me."

Delaney chewed her tongue, squelching the urge to smile.

"Cut it out," Sam said. "You're going to be putting out Sunday dinners until Satan himself is wearing snowshoes." But there was a tender tone beneath the irritation that tugged at Delaney.

Etta's frown deepened. "Ah. Stubborn as your father," she snapped, her voice not in the least weak, and clumped the rest of the way to the golf cart. "Watch yourself, Samson, or I'll start making you do your own laundry like a grown man ought. Drive me home," she ordered Delaney.

"I'll drive you, Etta."

She lifted her cane and planted it in the center of his chest, warding him off. "Your wife can drive me." Without waiting for comment from either Sam or Delaney, she climbed in the cart and situated her cane and purse. "Well? Are you going to sit here long enough to get a suntan or are you going to drive this thing?"

"Etta," Sam's voice held a warning.

"I'm not talking to you, Samson. Not until you come to see me under *my* roof."

"So be it," he agreed. "Don't be pushing on Delaney's gas pedal with that cane," he warned as he headed back inside his office. The door closed behind him, the blinds swinging in the window.

"Stubborn cuss," Etta grumbled.

"Might be a family trait," Delaney observed mildly as she set the cart in motion. It was embarrassing to realize how relieved she felt that *Etta* was the one doing his wash. She kept an eye on Etta's cane sitting across the woman's lap…just in case. The woman's wizened hand was gripped around it.

Etta harrumphed. But she didn't disagree. "Well, now, you can just tell me what kind of game you and Sam are playing at."

She ought to have been prepared for the direct attack. "There's no game," she said after a moment. The woman *was* Sam's grandmother; she deserved some sort of explanation, no matter what Sam had said about staying out of his family's business. "We're trying to rectify some mistakes we've made." That was diplomatic enough, wasn't it?

"Sam's unforgiving of mistakes. More in himself than others."

She steered the cart to the side of the road to avoid an enormous pothole. "I know."

Etta fell silent for a moment. Delaney was rather nervously aware of the way the woman's fingers toyed with her cane. She sped up a little, just in case.

"Do you love him?"

Her family never probed so blatantly. Of course, *her* family never had conversations that really mattered, either. It was one of the things that had propelled her into her profession. "I—"

"That's why you married him, isn't it? Stop!"

Delaney hit the brakes, startled right out of her wits. The cart shimmied and skidded sideways a foot. So did her heartbeat. "What's wrong?"

Etta set her gaze on Delaney. "Hemming and hawing. Do you love him or not?"

Etta would have done better to ask that question of Sam. His answer would have explained quite a lot. "Sometimes love isn't enough."

"You're a shrink, aren't you?"

"I'm a psychiatrist, yes."

"Then you ought to know that sometimes love is all there is." Etta shook her head, clearly disgusted. She climbed from the cart and settled her handbag over her arm. "You get Sam here on Sunday."

She *was* a psychiatrist. She was supposed to be good at dealing with people and conflict and feelings and all the reasons, physiological or not, that drove them. So why couldn't she summon a coherent response to Etta's order?

She just sat there, her fingers strangling the steering wheel, and watched Etta pick her way across the grass toward her rambling house.

She didn't drive away until Etta was safely inside, and even when Delaney arrived at Sam's house, she hadn't thought of a suitable response.

She unloaded the bag of groceries and found the minimum utensils to put together one of the few meals she actually knew how to make—oven-baked chicken, green salad and an apple crisp.

Then she sat at the bar and picked up the phone. She called her father first at the care center, but he didn't answer, and she left a message on his voice mail that she'd called to say hello. She called her mother second, but she didn't answer, either. One of the nameless maids that paraded through Jessica Townsend's home picked up. She left a message there, too, even though she knew her mother was unlikely to return the call. She never did.

Then, knowing that she'd been putting it off, she called Chad's private line. He answered almost immediately. They talked about patients, and they talked about the weather. They did not talk about the fact that she was staying under Sam's roof. And when she heard the front door open, something inside her jumped. A something that had never jumped with any other man.

She quickly ended the call, promising to check in later in the week.

"Do-Wright, I presume." Sam entered the kitchen,

his dark gaze going from the phone to her. "It's a wonder he hasn't trooped down here to rescue you from my evil clutches."

"I called Chad to check on my patients," she said truthfully. "I *am* neglecting them to stay down here, you know."

The dimple slashing down his cheek deepened, but he made no comment. He went over to the oven and opened the door. "You're cooking."

"Apparently." She felt defensive.

"Why?"

"I don't know. Hungry, perhaps? Maybe I wanted to see how it felt cooking in a kitchen that's a chef's dream."

"Can't believe you'd even contemplate marrying him. He'll bore you to death."

"Whereas you were never boring," Delaney murmured. "I'm not marrying him."

Sam nudged the ring box on the counter. "Not yet, anyway."

"What's the problem between you and your father?"

"Etta didn't tell you?"

"I didn't ask her."

"Now there's a switch. Dr. Townsend *not* asking questions."

"It's Dr. Vega, actually." She realized she was eyeing the head of lettuce still sitting on the counter, wondering if it would provide a nice heft should she heave it at his head. "It has been for two years now." She pushed her lips into a smile. "I used Townsend when I began communications with Annie and Logan Drake because I didn't want the name to become an issue where Alonso was concerned." The buzzer on the oven went off, an oddly appropriate coda to her statement.

She moved past him to turn it off. Then she pulled the chicken from the oven and set it on top of the range. "Enjoy the chicken, Sam. I find I've lost my appetite."

She set down the oven mitt and walked from the kitchen.

"By the way," she said before she turned down the hallway. "Happy anniversary."

Chapter 13

She'd remembered.

Sam swirled the amber liquid in his short squat glass before tossing it back. It held a satisfying burn as he swallowed.

But—unlike Delaney seemed to believe—he hadn't forgotten what day it was, either.

Their second anniversary. In a marriage that had been spent more apart than together.

He held up his hand. The wedding ring he'd given her glinted on the tip of his little finger.

He thumped the glass on his nightstand and pushed off his bed. It was nearly midnight. Nearly the end of the day, the end of their second anniversary. The only anniversary they'd ever spent under the same roof.

On their first anniversary, Sam had gone to San Diego, gotten drunk and slept it off in a five-hundred dollar a night hotel room.

The door to her bedroom was closed. He pushed it open.

The light on the nightstand cast a soft glow across the bed. Delaney was in bed, her back propped up on the two pillows. Her open briefcase sat on the bed beside her. Case files—once neatly stacked on her lap—had slid sideways onto the mattress. She had a pen in her slack fingers, gold-framed reading glasses on her nose and wore a thin, sleeveless white T-shirt that hugged her curves more closely than a lover.

She was asleep.

He rubbed his hand down his mouth, then around the back of his neck. How many nights had she come to bed with work just this way?

Hell, for that matter, how many times had he been called out on a case when they'd had dinner plans, or any other plans?

He crossed the room and carefully lifted the files from her lap and the bed. He stacked them together and set them inside the briefcase. He slid the gold pen from her hand and tucked it next to the matching pencil in the slot. Being careful not to jostle the bed, he lifted the open case and set it on the dresser.

Delaney hadn't moved.

He let his eyes take his fill of her. Over the gilded sheen of her hair, down the creamy length of her throat to the shadowy cleavage revealed by the scooped neck of the thin, ribbed shirt.

He exhaled sharply. He needed his head examined. Or a dip in the ocean to cool his jets. He approached the side of her bed again and barely touching her, slid the glasses from her nose. He set them on the nightstand, then reached for the lamp.

"Sam?" Her voice was soft. Thick with sleep. As different from the raw tone of her "Happy anniversary" as a voice could get, and it reached down inside him, clamping like a tight velvet fist.

"Go back to sleep."

In a sinuous motion, she slid down the pillows. The sheet dragged down around her hips where the bottom of the shirt had ridden up, displaying a pale slice of flesh. She languidly lifted her arms in the same way she'd done when he'd had to leave their bed because of some case he was working.

Desire slammed into need.

Need warred with common sense.

She was asleep.

But at least she hadn't murmured Do-Wright's name. He went on his knees beside the bed, throwing out common sense the same way he always did when it came to Delaney. His hands slid over the supple strength of her biceps.

Any minute she'd wake up and give him hell.

Maybe it'd be worth it.

She sighed and turned more fully toward him, her hands curving over his shoulders as he leaned over her.

In a movement achingly familiar, she flattened one hand against his back, the other sank into his hair, and her nose found the crook of his neck.

Crown him king of idiots.

He nudged. She turned. And instead of just being hunched over the bed, he was lying alongside her on top of it. Her knee slid over his leg. She was boneless, thoroughly asleep.

He couldn't make the same claim.

Definitely king of idiots.

He scooped her up until she lay on top of him. He cupped her face between his hands. Murmured her name.

Her eyes popped open.

Her lips parted in a silent "oh" as the sleep cleared from those deep pools of blue.

Only then did he kiss her.

Resistance was fleeting. Then her hands pulled, rather than pushed. Her knees fell to either side of him, her fingertips grazed his jaw, his temple. He ran his hands over the flare of her hips. The shirt was no barrier when his fingers tunneled beneath it, exploring the silk of her back right up to her shoulder blades.

She dragged her mouth from his, planted her hand on his chest and pushed herself up. Her hair tumbled forward over her cheeks, her eyes. He could feel the imprint of her slender hand splayed against his chest, as if it were dipped in fire. The warm weight of her sitting on his thighs was a torture all its own.

"I don't understand you." She whispered, but the admission settled on him like daggers. "I don't know what you want from me."

Everything. Nothing. He closed his eyes against the sight of her, against the swell of her breasts, rosy crests thrusting against the thin cotton. *Nothing* would be easier, but it was also empty. Dull. Lifeless.

And he was still alive, as her arrival on Turnabout had pointedly reminded him.

He jackknifed, keeping her in place on his lap, until his nose was inches from hers. "I'm hard, and I'm tired of games. What the hell did you come here for, Laney? The pleasure of stripping my skin right off me? 'Cause that's what it's like having you near and not *having* you."

"You're the one who's kept me a virtual prisoner on this island."

"I'm not talking about that." It took more effort than he liked to keep his voice from rising. "And short of locking you in one of my jail cells, we both know there's not a place on this earth that you couldn't stroll in or out of if you were so inclined."

"Oh, right. As if I can arrange my life in whatever fashion suits me? You're describing my mother, Sam. Not me."

The hell of it was, he knew she was right. Delaney had never traded on Jessica Townsend's wealth or name. Nor had she done so on her father's reputation with the force. Two people who could offer everything to her but who hadn't.

Yet Delaney had survived. Hell, she'd even excelled.

She hadn't needed her parents any more than she'd needed him. "And if you *could* arrange it, what would you do?"

Her lashes swept down, hiding those deep, soft pools. Then she looked at him. "Are you sure you want to know the answer to that?"

Don't ask the question if you're not prepared to listen to the answer. How many times had he heard her voice that belief?

He lifted her from him and rolled off the bed. Her gaze drifted over him, clung in places that only served to make him more annoyed. With her. With himself. With the past, and most particularly with the present. "Look somewhere else, Delaney, unless you really want the answer to *that.*"

Color rioted in her cheeks. She didn't look away.

He leaned over her, planting his hands on the mattress. The muscles in her long, elegant throat worked in a swallow. He knew if he kissed her again, they'd spend the rest of the night tearing apart the bed.

The knowledge made him even harder. But he flipped the ring off his finger and held it in front of her. "Why'd you bring this back?"

Her lips pressed together for a moment. "I always thought it was an unusual band," she murmured. "I didn't realize how unusual until I drove Etta home. It's a family ring, isn't it? You didn't go out and buy it. She wears one just like it."

He didn't deny it. *"Why?"*

She sighed a little. "What does it matter, Sam? You were so ashamed of us that you kept our marriage a secret from your own family."

"I was never ashamed of you."

"Then why? You didn't think our marriage had a chance of working, so why tell anyone?"

"Yes."

She blanched. "Well. I guess I asked the right question. How…embarrassing."

"Stop."

"Why?" She pushed at him and slid across the bed, away from him. "You married me, but you didn't expect it to work. Why did you even bother talking me into Las Vegas? We were responsible adults, Sam, more than capable of dealing with my pregnancy—"

"Because your dad was a jerk. Because he couldn't see past his nose to stop blaming you for something your brother caused. Because your mother was more interested in screwing her Russian mobster-gardener than being a mother when you needed one. Because—"

"You felt sorry for me." She looked away, her expression pained. "Dandy," he heard her whisper.

"Because you were beautiful and too good for the son of a criminal," he corrected flatly. "And nothing about that has changed. Not even if you're pregnant now."

"What are you talking about?"

"Danté," he bit out, "is a convicted felon."

"So? I saw his ankle bracelet earlier, Sam. I'm not an idiot. I've had dozens of patients who wore bracelets just like it. Your father's on house arrest. That's why he wasn't at Maisy's barbecue on the beach, and the only time I've seen him in town was with you."

"Parole, to be accurate. And everybody expects apples not to fall far from the tree."

She eyed him, seeming to forget that she wore only a thin T-shirt and panties cut high on her mile-long legs.

"My father was a cop. A good one. Randy was a total screwup, into everything not necessarily shy of illegal. They still loved each other. *What has that got to do with you and me?*"

"Danté is a forger. My whole life was colored by his deeds. He was good but not good enough to not get caught. Again and again and again. Even by me. You know what it feels like to have to arrest your own father?"

Her brows drew together. "Oh, Sam."

"You wouldn't have had dinner with me if you'd known about him, much less married me. Christ, Delaney, your mother is an heiress. Your dad was a cop. *They* didn't make it work. How were we supposed to make it work?"

"They split up after the accident! Neither one of them handled Randy's death well."

"So they split and managed to forget that not all of their children died that night when Randy drove you both off the road."

She winced but didn't deny the truth of his words, "You could have told me about Danté, Sam. You *chose* not to. Do you think so little of me?"

"What I *think* is that you didn't want to be there in the first place and any excuse—"

"You should have told me." Her voice rose sharply.

"When would I have done so, Delaney? Maybe made an appointment with your secretary so I could see you?"

She jerked as if he'd slapped her.

"You spent nearly twenty hours a day at the office," he went on, his voice tight. He tossed the wedding ring on the bed. "You married me, but you didn't want to be around me. There was nothing you needed from me. I may not be a doctor of psychiatry, but even *I* picked up on *that*."

"You're wrong." Her voice was hoarse.

But he knew he wasn't. "You were the princess in the ivory tower. Only, you kept sneaking down. Kept taking pro bono cases, cases that nobody else wanted to deal with. Getting your hands in the muck and the mire of a world that wasn't pretty at all. Why was that? Because you thought if you did your father might recognize that he hadn't lost everything in the accident you and Randy had? That your brother may have died, but you were alive and important, too?"

It took the sight of tears rolling down her cheeks to stop his tirade. She'd never cried easily. Not in the two years he'd known her before they'd eloped. Not in the four months they'd been together before he'd chucked it all and walked out, leaving his personal life in even more shambles than his professional one.

But with the anger gone, it left a gaping hole inside him. One that was too damned familiar and too damned painful.

When she finally spoke, her voice was barely audible. "Does Danté's record have something to do with you losing your job?"

Why not? Of course she'd make the obvious connection. "The money was counterfeit. It had Danté's artistry all over it. When the money disappeared from the evidence locker, they blamed *me*."

"But you wouldn't—"

"Are you *sure* about that, Laney?" His jaw was so tight it ached. "That day in the hospital when I told you about Internal Affairs calling me in, you didn't even question it. What would you have thought if you'd known about Danté?"

"The only thing I was thinking that day was that I was never going to hold our baby in my arms." Her eyes were red. "That when I'd needed you with me, you weren't there. And that the very reason you'd married me no longer existed. You blamed me for going out that night to pick up Alonso, and you never stopped. Then two weeks later you moved out, proving that I was right."

"I moved out because you couldn't bring yourself to look me in the face. Because if I hadn't been so determined to follow every goddamned letter of the law, I would have gone myself, and you'd have never been driving in the first place!"

She pressed the back of her hand to her mouth, her head shaking. Tears dripped down her cheeks. "I didn't blame you for my accident," she finally whispered.

"And I didn't blame you for it, either."

She gingerly lowered herself to the foot of the bed, her head bowed, her soft hair falling on either side of her neck.

There were so many things about Delaney that had gotten to him. But the most damaging had been the vulnerability she tried so damned hard to hide.

"The money was found, eventually," he said abruptly.

"My record was cleared. But I knew I wasn't going back to New York again."

"Because of me."

He exhaled roughly. Pulled the handkerchief from his back pocket and handed it to her. "Yes."

She was silent for a long moment. But she finally took the square of cloth and pressed it to her eyes. "You're the only man I know who carries a handkerchief." Her voice was muffled. Careful.

"Comes from being raised by an annoying grandmother." His voice was just as careful.

"She loves you."

He'd never doubted it. Maybe Delaney had been born to a woman who could buy and sell half of Manhattan. But he'd been the one to know someone in his life loved him even if she did cause him no end of consternation. "She's big on family."

"Something she obviously passed on to you." Her voice was husky. "She wants you to go to dinner on Sunday."

"She always does. She knows why I won't."

"Because of your father."

"Yes."

She tilted back her head. Her eyes were red. Her nose was red. Her lips were full.

He was still a hairbreadth away from tumbling her back on the bed.

"Some anniversary, hmm?" Her lips twisted in a macabre stab at humor.

Unfortunately, he'd been known to have a touch of the macabre himself. One of the ways a detective managed to stay sane in the city. "Like none I've ever had before." Ironic truth.

"I spent last year's working." Her fingers curled into her palms, surrounding the handkerchief. "I didn't need to. I just…didn't want to go home."

"Was Chad there?" He hated the question; the lack of control he had in asking it.

"He would have been if I'd asked." She glanced at him, then looked away. "I didn't ask. I didn't want Chad. I've never wanted Chad. Not that way. If I had, I could have married him ten years ago, the first time he asked."

"But you considered it." It wasn't a question. How could it be, when he knew the answer.

She inhaled. Exhaled. Stood and held out the cloth to him. "I thought it was the smart thing to do."

He didn't take the cloth, and her hand finally lowered. "And you've always prided yourself on being smart."

She turned away, but he could still see her face in the mirror. "When brains are a person's only strength? Yes."

"None of this changes the fact that you could be pregnant."

In the mirror's reflection he saw her eyes close, her fingers curl until her knuckles were white. "I won't be." Her voice was raw. "But I'll wait it out just to satisfy you."

He stepped behind her, closing his hands over her shoulders. Looking at their reflections. He, tanned and dark-haired; she, ivory-skinned and fair. Her gaze met his in the mirror and it was filled with emotions he couldn't even put a name to.

"Get some sleep," he said after a moment. "Midnight has passed. Celebrating is done."

Her eyes flickered. "I'm sorry."

He drew his thumbs down the curve of her shoulders, and away. "So am I." About so many things.

Leaving the ring on the bed, he walked out of the room and closed the door behind him.

He wished he could close the door on his feelings where she was concerned as easily.

Chapter 14

"Have you seen Caitlin?" Annie poked her head in the playroom, where Delaney was reading a story to Mary.

Delaney shook her head. Mary did, too.

Annie nodded and disappeared.

Delaney smiled down at the little girl, transferring the picture book into her hands. "Keep reading. I'll be back." She climbed to her feet and hurried after Annie. "Is something wrong?"

"Caitlin's gone missing." Annie kept her voice low as she walked toward the front of the house. "Alonso was the one who noticed first. I've looked everywhere for her. Logan went off-island this morning to talk to someone who's applied for Dr. Weathers's position. I've called Sam. He's on his way over."

Her stomach sank. Not entirely because of Caitlin.

She and Sam may have finally spoken about matters that should have been addressed earlier, but since their abysmal anniversary a week ago, they'd gone out of their way to avoid each other. He'd be gone from the house when she woke, and she'd be gone when he returned. And Sunday had passed without one mention of Etta's dinner.

"Maybe she went to see the father of her baby."

Annie shook her head. "Whoever that is. But she'd have had to cross the same time Logan did. She didn't."

"So she's still on Turnabout. Has she done this kind of thing before?"

"No." She raked her fingers through her hair, looking clearly rattled. "Why would she run away?"

"Did she have an argument with anyone here?"

Annie kept shaking her head. "She spends a lot of her time with Alonso. You've surely noticed that."

Delaney had. She'd spent so much time with the residents of Castillo House that Annie and Logan had taken to joking that they needed to build her a bedroom, too. "Does Betty have any ideas?"

Again another head shake.

"She got pregnant by a cop, you know." Alonso stood in the great room watching them. "I'm pretty sure of it. That's why she doesn't like the sheriff much."

Annie pressed her palm to her stomach. "If she wants to see the father of her baby, all she'd have to do is say so. We'd help her."

"She doesn't want to see the guy. She doesn't want to—" He broke off.

"Alonso." Delaney reached up and caught his face, gently forcing him to look at her. "If you know something, now's the time to say so."

"She didn't tell me nothing," Alonso insisted. "Honest."

She narrowed her eyes, studying him. "But you have some idea, yes?"

"She said she wanted to be alone. That she knew there was one place she could be sure of it. She's scared of havin' the kid, you know? She said she wished she were a bird, so she could just fly off and be alone."

"One place? On the island?"

"Yeah. She likes being outside. You know how she's always talking about birds. And that's all I know."

Delaney nodded. "Okay. Why don't you go make sure the children keep occupied?" She waited until he'd left, then turned back to Annie just as Sam came through the front door.

His dark gaze went from her to Annie. "Found her yet?"

Annie shook her head and relayed what Alonso had said.

Delaney tugged at her lower lip. "I'm worried about the 'fly away' comment." She looked at Annie. "Has Caitlin exhibited any signs of harming herself or the baby?" Just because she hadn't seen any didn't mean that it wasn't occurring.

"No. She's been increasingly emotional the farther along she gets, but I didn't think it was out of the ordinary, given her situation. She's not due for another six weeks or so." She pressed her hand to her mouth for a moment. "This is my fault. I should have seen something sooner."

"Don't do that, Annie," Sam spoke finally. "If anybody understands her, it'd be you. Sit tight. Delaney and I will go look for her. She hasn't left Turnabout. We'll find her."

His calm words obviously reassured Annie, though they set off alarms all throughout Delaney. But there was no thought on her part of refusing to help. So she squeezed Annie's hand reassuringly and followed Sam out to his truck.

But once they'd driven over half the island, searched out every cranny where Sam thought Caitlin might be bird-watching, his words of assurance had worn thin.

"Alonso's probably sending us on some damn goose chase," Sam muttered. "He and Caitlin are sitting back somewhere having a laugh at us."

"Alonso wouldn't do that." Delaney scanned the landscape.

"End of the road." Sam's voice was bland. They had come to the end of the road. Literally. His truck bounced over the uneven terrain. "Only thing out this way is Luis's Point."

"That's the place your father mentioned."

"It's the cliff Luis Castillo jumped from a million years ago. Because his fiancée betrayed him with his best friend, Henry Fielding. It's supposedly the start of the Turnabout curse." He shook his head, looking disgusted. "The Point's been a popular place lately. That's where Teddy and Vern Haggerty were brawling when I got this." He gestured at his bruised cheekbone. It had begun turning interesting shades of green and yellow.

"Take us there."

"Laney—"

"Please, Sam." Delaney closed her hand over his arm. "Alonso wouldn't lie about Caitlin. She's pregnant and he wouldn't—"

"Ah, hell. There she is." Sand and gravel spewed beneath the tires when Sam veered.

"Where? I don't see anything." Only boulders and scrub and the ocean far beyond it.

"Trust me." The truck fishtailed to a stop. Delaney got out, following Sam as he made his way to the edge of the cliff. She scrambled between bushes that caught at the soft fabric of the knit shorts she wore. Her feet in the tennis shoes Sam had procured slid over rocks and around boulders.

Then she stopped short and sucked in her shock.

Caitlin *was* there. Below the edge of the cliff, perched on a sort of shelf that protruded out over the ocean.

Dizziness pushed in on her.

Tires squealing.

Falling.

Keep it together, Laney.

She focused. "How did you even spot her?"

"You have to talk to her," he said. "Get her off the shelf. Or at least get her to move back so I can grab her."

"Sam, I don't—" Her throat went tight, choking off the words.

He folded his hands over hers. "Look at me." He

squeezed tighter, until she did as he bade. And his eyes looked into hers, seeming to will her roiling stomach to quiet. "You're not going over the edge," he said calmly. "You're going to keep Caitlin safe. This is what you do, right? You help kids. You always have." He leaned over her, his voice soft. Steady. "There's plenty of space on the ledge. It's wider than the deck on my house, and you've been out there and been just fine."

She shook her head. "You should do this."

"I'm the law. She hates me." As he spoke, Sam led her along the cliff, closer to the point above Caitlin. "I'll be right above you."

Sam was right. She knew it. She forced herself to let go of his hand, steadying herself as she made her way down the incline to the shelf where Caitlin stood poised.

"Caitlin." She didn't want to startle the girl, even though Caitlin had to have heard her noisy descent. "Hey, there. Seeing any unusual birds?"

"Only seagulls." The girl's words were barely audible.

Delaney pointed at a small object in the sky. It dipped toward the water then shot up again, a miracle against gravity. "They really are pretty to watch, aren't they? Even if they are just seagulls."

Caitlin bowed her head over her swollen abdomen, cradling her arms against herself. "I can't do this."

"Okay." Delaney inched forward another half foot.

Caitlin's head lifted, she frowned. "Don't come any closer. I'll jump, I swear it."

"Okay." Delaney didn't dare look up at Sam. She just glanced around at the uneven rocks. "I'm gonna sit down here, though. Right here. For a few minutes. The, um, the height makes me a little dizzy. Then I'll leave you alone. Okay?" There was no need to playact. The drop from the cliff was staggering. No matter what Sam said, being on this cliff was considerably different from sitting behind the safety rail on his deck.

She cautiously lowered herself to the ground, and felt a little more secure once she did.

"I don't want *him* here."

Because Sam represented the law. As in the cop who'd gotten her—a minor—pregnant. Delaney couldn't even let herself think about that particular situation at the moment. So she went for lightness. "Who? Sam? I don't want him here, either." She didn't need to look up to know he was there. Alert. "He's annoying that way, I'm afraid. Ignore him. He won't mind. Doesn't faze him." Too bad she couldn't seem to follow her own advice.

Caitlin's reddened gaze slid Delaney's way. "You're married to him."

"Yes." Delaney planted the heels of her shoes more firmly on the rocks, hoping they'd provide enough of a break to keep her from sliding any closer to the edge. "As it turns out. Annie's been looking for you everywhere. Everyone's worried about you. Alonso. Mary. All of them."

Caitlin made an odd sound, her young face so skeptical it made Delaney hurt inside. "Alonso doesn't even hardly know me."

"He knows enough to think you're nice. He wouldn't

have helped you with the math, otherwise. Believe me." She smiled a little, hoping the girl would relax.

Caitlin sucked in the corner of her lip, her forehead crinkling. "Nice. Right. I should'a got rid of it a long time ago." She pressed her palm to her pregnant belly.

"But you didn't." Delaney kept her voice gentle, but matter-of-fact as she followed the girl's lead. "Have you talked with anyone about your options?"

Caitlin hesitated. "Annie. Dr. Weathers."

Delaney knew that, of course. But she wanted to keep Caitlin talking. She wanted to know what Caitlin wasn't saying, because that was undoubtedly more important than what she *had*. "But it's hard to decide what's right, isn't it."

"I don't wanna be a mom!" Caitlin looked miserable. She rocked back and forth on the balls of her swollen feet. Restless. Her hands went from her abdomen to the small of her back, pressing through her pale yellow dress.

"Do you think you have to be?"

"My mom had kids," Caitlin mumbled, "every year another one. And now they're all gone." She winced, swearing under her breath. Casting a look up at Sam, as if afraid he'd break out his cuffs because she'd cursed.

"You don't have to decide anything right now, Caitlin."

"Yes, I do!"

Delaney folded her hands together to keep from reaching out for the girl. "Why?"

Caitlin rocked. Back and forth. Then she finally shot Delaney a look. "Because I think I'm in labor."

They both heard Sam's muffled oath.

Their perch on the cliff shrank by mammoth proportions. Delaney forced her voice to remain calm. "Are you having contractions?"

The girl didn't answer. She looked out over the roiling water far below.

"Caitlin." Delaney pushed to her feet. They were several feet from the edge of the cliff. Yards. She relaxed her throat, drawing in a slow breath. Her vision wasn't pinpointing. She was needed. "Caitlin? For how long now?"

"Since yesterday. I thought it was just my back hurting."

Yesterday. Good Lord. Delaney slowly stepped closer to the girl. Sam was right above them. Silent but steady. A rock of a different sort. "You're not going to jump, Caitlin. You don't want to. If you did, you wouldn't have told Alonso anything. You don't have to decide anything right now about your future or the baby's future. The only thing you need to do right now is let Sam and me help you off this cliff."

"Oh, God," Caitlin looked down at herself, her face wrinkling. "What—"

Delaney stared, too. For only a moment, though. She'd have time to panic later. "Your water broke." She kept her voice matter-of-fact. It wasn't easy. "Come on, Caitlin, give me your hand. That baby wants to be born. Soon. So let's get you somewhere a little more comfortable than this piece of granite."

Caitlin hunched forward, perilously close to the drop-off. "It hurts."

Delaney cast a look up at Sam and felt a little calmer.

He was above Caitlin on the other side of her. "I know, Caitlin. Just take one step back toward me. Give me your hand. We'll help you the rest of the way."

Only, Caitlin cried out, pitching forward onto her knees.

Delaney darted to her, wrapping her arms around her shoulders. The girl felt rigid. She was bracing herself against the pain. Delaney slid her hand into Caitlin's, her mouth close to the girl's ear. "Don't fight it, baby. Just ride it out. Breathe with me. It'll pass in a minute. Breathe. That's it. Good girl."

Caitlin exhaled roughly. She shuddered.

"Sam—" Delaney turned around to look for him, but he was already beside them.

Murmuring quietly to Caitlin, he slipped his hands under her and picked her right up.

Delaney held her breath, closed her eyes for a brief second. So close to the edge. Too close. The sound of water overwhelmed her. Birds crying, waves crashing, hot sunlight, salty air.

"Laney."

She started. Looked at Sam. His dark eyes were steady, meeting hers. Panic receded.

"Go first," he said. Caitlin huddled against him—testament to her pain that she accepted his help—her limbs painfully slender in contrast to her swollen abdomen.

"No." Delaney shook her head, turning to face the abbreviated climb. "I'm okay. I'll follow you. Go."

He didn't wait around to argue. Rocks crunched beneath his boots, a small showering avalanche of shifting footholds. Delaney focused on his back, following, pressing her palm against the small of his back when he hesitated.

"Contraction," he said.

No two people had ever felt, so acutely, someone else's pain. Delaney's fingers curled into the fabric of Sam's shirt. His body heat blazed.

"Okay," Caitlin said an eternity later. Her voice was faint. Breathless.

The trio moved upward. More quickly as Sam neared more level ground. Then his long strides ate up the distance to his truck.

Delaney ran alongside. Caitlin cried out again. Barely a break between contractions. Sam caught her gaze. She swallowed, and instead of opening the passenger door to his truck, she went to the back and dragged open the tailgate. Thank goodness it was an SUV. The cargo area was carpeted and would be somewhat softer.

"There's a first-aid kit under the driver's seat." He settled Caitlin while Delaney ran around to retrieve it.

She clambered over the seats and handed it to him. He set it down beside Caitlin where it looked woefully insubstantial. "Can't you call Dr. Hugo?"

"He's off-island for a few days. There's a blanket in the backseat."

Delaney grabbed it. Reached over the seat to hand it to him, as well. "Off-island! When are his few days done?"

"I can't have the baby." Caitlin's voice was strangled. "It's too early!"

"Sure you can," Sam said easily. "You're young,

you're healthy and you'll feel a helluva lot better when you're through."

Delaney bit her lip, catching the very definite roll of Caitlin's eyes. But it was cut off by another contraction that had her curling forward, her lips parted over a hissing pant. What seemed an eternity later, her head fell back again. "I need a doctor," she wailed.

"Delaney *is* a doctor."

Delaney's jaw loosened. But she swallowed her protest when Caitlin looked up at her with painful relief. "Right. I'm a doctor." The fact that she'd never once delivered a baby—something Sam knew good and well— was a moot point. She got out of the truck and hurried around to the back. For Caitlin's sake, she'd stay calm even if it killed her.

But later she might well do in Sam.

Praying that this would go as smoothly as Sam's attitude suggested, she helped Caitlin get as comfortable as possible. There wasn't much time for preparations. Shaking with tension, she pawed through the first-aid kit. There was a silver-colored emergency blanket folded into a ridiculously small square. She ripped open the packet and spread it out atop the blanket. She'd barely managed to pull on the packet of sterile gloves before Caitlin hunched forward in one continuous contraction.

Sam abruptly suggested driving them to town, but Delaney shook her head. "The baby's crowning." Her voice was high—nearly as panicked as Caitlin's had been. Then Caitlin turned the air blue with curses, and the baby slid into Delaney's shaking hands.

She stared into the little scrunched-up face for a moment. Some long-ago teaching had her tilting the baby's head slightly lower than his feet. He was so tiny. So vulnerable. So perfect as his face pinkened and his little mouth parted.

He wailed.

"What about the cord?" Sam's voice broke her trance. His hands rifled through the first aid kit.

Delaney huffed the hair out of her eyes. The umbilical cord was still pulsing. "Find something to tie the cord—two places."

"Is it a boy like Dr. Hugo said?" Caitlin pushed herself weakly up on her elbows.

"Yes."

She collapsed back once more. "Is he supposed to cry like that?"

"He's fine, Caitlin." Delaney hoped. "He's beautiful."

"There's nothing in here to tie it with," Sam pushed aside the kit, his own face looking pale.

Delaney smoothed her hands over the baby, calming. "Your shoelace," she said.

Sam quickly untied his boot and dragged the long leather lacing from it. "It should be cleaner," he muttered. "When do we do this? Where?"

The cord had stopped pulsing. "Now. Four inches from the baby," she murmured for his ears only. "A few inches above that. Cut between."

His fingers worked fast. Nimbly. The first-aid kit might not be equipped for childbirth, but it did have an adequate pair of scissors. As soon as he cut the cord, he dropped the scissors on the silvery sheet and grabbed a corner of the blanket that was still clean and ripped it clean away.

Emotions tangled inside her as—between the two of them—they wrapped the baby in the torn blanket.

Delaney caught Sam's gaze on her. Her throat tightened. She settled the squalling baby in his arms and hastily turned her attention back to tending Caitlin. But she was excruciatingly aware of Sam holding the infant.

He'd married her because she'd been pregnant, but she'd never doubted that he hadn't wanted the baby.

It was *her* he hadn't wanted.

"Let me hold him." Caitlin's voice was tired. Young. Scared.

Sam handed over the baby to Caitlin, settling him on her chest because the girl was exhausted. He stayed close, yet managed not to hover. An uncommon skill.

Delaney looked away, concentrating on cleaning up as best she could. *This* was the Sam who was the most dangerous.

The kind Sam. The gentle Sam.

"We should get them both some medical attention," she said, when she was sure her voice would work.

"I'll check with Sara. She might know when her dad is getting back. Otherwise, I'll get a chopper here to take them to the mainland."

"You prob'ly wish Annie and Logan woulda done that sooner." Caitlin peered down at the baby.

"And miss this?" Delaney shook her head and climbed

in beside the teen so Sam could drive them back to town. "Not a chance."

Caitlin's lips twitched. Then her faint smile died and she looked away.

The truck rocked as Sam slowly drove back toward the road. Delaney put out a hand to help Caitlin hold the baby steady, and she saw the tears leaking from the girl's closed eyes. "You don't have to decide anything until you're ready, Caitlin," she assured gently. "And you're not alone in this."

"My mom's dead."

Delaney smoothed back Caitlin's tangle of damp hair. "I wasn't talking about your mom."

Caitlin didn't reply. Sam made it to the road, and the ride smoothed considerably. In minutes, he'd pulled up outside a colorful house with a sign hanging from the eve that said Doctor. "Wait here," he said as he got out of the truck.

Caitlin finally opened her eyes, glancing up at Delaney. "What? He thinks we're gonna go surfing or something?"

Delaney smiled faintly. But her gaze was on Sam as he strode up the porch steps and ducked to avoid a dangling wind chime.

He looked back, and Delaney quickly averted her gaze. But her heart raced, all the same.

Was there ever a bigger fool than she was?

To have fallen in love with her own husband all over again?

Chapter 15

"How do you think she'll do?"

Delaney hesitated at Sam's question. They'd just watched the helicopter take off into the sunset from the cleared space outside of Castillo House. It carried Caitlin, the baby and Betty Weathers, who'd jumped at the chance of leaving the island.

"Caitlin's fine. The baby seems to be fine, too. Despite being early. But how do I think she'll *do?*" She lifted one shoulder. She was tired right down to her bones. "I don't know. She's only seventeen. She has no family left, which, of course, is how she came to be at Castillo House. Another year and she could be out on her own, going to school, working. But with a baby?" She shook her head. "I don't know."

"You think she should give him up?"

"What I think doesn't matter. It's a choice Caitlin will have to make."

"Yet you just said she's a kid."

"I said she was very young to have so much responsibility on her plate. And then, of course, there's the matter of who the baby's father is. Alonso said he thinks he was a cop."

Sam's eyes narrowed. He realized the implication of that as much as she did. Caitlin was underage. A police officer would not be. "But not who?"

"No." She rubbed her eyes, knowing any semblance of makeup she'd once possessed was long gone.

"We need to get you some dinner."

The comment came out of left field, halting her automatic gear into debate over what Alonso did and did not say. "Oh."

"Aren't you hungry?"

Her stomach growled. Loudly. Right on cue. And Sam's lips tilted. Delaney felt her face heat. There was plenty of space between them in the clearing, yet just then Delaney was acutely aware of him. His presence. His height. His warmth.

The fact that he'd made her come alive after more than twenty-one cold months.

She chewed the inside of her lip. "I haven't had a chance to thank you." She needed to get the conversation back on *her* footing. "I mean, to thank you for everything you did today for Caitlin."

"What I did for Caitlin wasn't unusual." He stepped

closer. Delaney had the distinct feeling that her control was only a notion in her mind, a notion that was as insubstantial as a grain of sand on a windswept beach. "Anybody would've helped her."

"Anybody didn't. *You* did. And I'm certain Caitlin appreciates it."

"So, if she comes back to Turnabout, maybe she won't cross the street to the other side when she sees me." He slid his fingers beneath the lock of hair falling over her eyebrow.

Delaney froze. "Sam—"

"Were you thinking about your brother out there? At Luis's Point. It probably brought it all back for you. The accident you and Randy had."

She didn't know what was worse. Having him probe her thoughts or having him stand so close her senses were filled with memories. Recent. Not-so-recent. It didn't matter; they were all alive in her mind, flowing in her veins. "Actually, what I was really thinking about was the other accident," she admitted.

His lids lowered, hiding his expression. "Yeah."

She gnawed on the inside of her lip. "I don't think I'm pregnant, Sam. But what are we going to do if I am?"

He didn't answer for a long while. "Hopefully a better job than we did before."

She felt like crying all over again. "You know it was a girl," she whispered. "The nurse told me."

His expression wasn't inscrutable now. It was ragged. "Jesus, Laney."

"I'm sorry." She dashed her fingers over her

cheeks. "I'm sorry. I don't know why I keep thinking about it. *Her*."

"It's called grieving." His voice seemed to come from deep inside him. "Maybe it's about time."

"Yes." She looked over at him. The sky behind him was turning from pink to fiery red. "Are you going to charge me for the therapy session?"

His mouth kicked up.

Silence settled between them. Except, for once, it wasn't tight with tension. It was simply…quiet.

And they stood there. Watching the sky.

When the sun finally hit the ocean in a blaze that ought to have bubbled the water, Delaney spoke. "Do you really like living here, Samson?"

She heard him sigh. "Yeah." Then he shook his head a little. "Amazingly enough, I do. This place here needs me. 'Turns' don't need much, but they need me a helluva lot more than I was ever needed in your dad's precinct. Or any other precinct for that matter." He angled a look her way. "You know what that's like. Your patients need you."

Her throat tightened. There was something distinctly different from her patients who required competent medical care and how Sam served the residents of Turnabout. She'd known other people who left practices in the city for small-town life. But she'd never once considered that it might be something she'd face.

Not that Sam wanted her to stay unless she was pregnant. And the chances of that were on a par with slim. If she were a braver woman she'd get a test done to prove it right now. "I'm a mess," she said abruptly. Literally and emotionally. "I'd like to clean up."

He nodded. They turned away from the vestige of sunset and headed back to the house where his truck was parked. "And then you're going to eat."

She was too tired and hungry to argue the statement.

Annie came out when they got to the house. She'd received word that the helicopter had already landed at the hospital in San Diego. She hugged Sam, then hugged Delaney, too. "Thanks for everything. You two were great today. You ought to talk Delaney into working here, Sam. Then Logan could stop interviewing."

Delaney chanced a glance at Sam at that. He pulled open the door for Delaney. "Anything to save Logan some work?"

Annie laughed a little. "It's all the paperwork involved. You know he hates it." She went back up the steps. "See you later."

They drove back to Sam's place in silence. When they went inside, she immediately headed to the shower. Sam, she knew, would go throw out some seeds for the birds and then would probably fix some food that he'd insist she eat even if she no longer felt hungry.

She closed the door to the bedroom and stripped off her soiled clothing, then padded into the attached bathroom and turned on the water. Ten seconds later she was standing beneath the steaming stream, letting it wash away her emotions until she felt numb again.

When she finally came out, she put on the plain white sundress and twisted her wet hair up with a clip. She tried not to look at the wedding band that she'd moved to the dresser after Sam had left it on her bed the night of their anniversary and went out to the kitchen.

The microwave was humming, and Sam *was* out on the deck. He seemed to prefer it to any other place in his house. She went over to the open door and looked out. The sky was as magnificent as he'd warned. A dome of silver-speckled black meeting a carpet of rippling silver-streaked black. "What's in the microwave?"

He jerked, looking grim. He'd obviously showered, too, and had changed. "Some chicken thing Janie brought over from Etta."

"What's wrong?"

He shoved back his wet hair and nudged her through the door into the kitchen. "Chad called while you were in the shower."

Chad. Not Do-Wright. "And?"

He frowned, hesitating.

Her nerves tightened warningly. "Sam?"

"Chad's been trying to reach you all day. Randall had another stroke. Last night."

Her stomach plunged further. *"And?"* The microwave softly pinged.

He just looked at her, and she knew, even before he said the words. "I'm sorry, Laney. He died. Chad said Jessica called him this morning looking for you. Apparently, the care center notified her last night when it happened. He said she's scheduled the funeral for the day after tomorrow."

"My father didn't have me listed to be notified," she

said faintly. And Jessica hadn't paid any heed to the messages she'd left with her whereabouts.

He drew his hand down the back of her head, threading through her hair. "I don't think I can get you to San Diego in time for any flights tonight."

She disentangled herself from him, moving around to the microwave that was continuing to ding. She opened it and pulled out the container. "Morning will be fine." Her voice was thin. "It's not like my father's going to miss me now. Obviously, Mother has already put her attorneys on the situation if she's already planned the funeral. They may have divorced eons ago, but they still considered each other next of kin. Just watch. She'll have a harpist and too many lilies and do exactly what my father would have hated."

Sam exhaled and pulled her back into his arms. "How much more can happen in one day?"

She leaned against him for a moment.

He tilted back her head, studying the misery she knew she couldn't hide. He lowered his mouth to hers. Her lips trembled. He kissed her temple. Her forehead. She inhaled shakily, his tenderness nearly undoing her.

"I wasn't there for him, Sam. He didn't want me, but I should have been there, anyway."

"For you or for him?" He caught a slow tear that leaked from the corner of her eye. "You never gave your father any reason to doubt your love for him. Don't blame yourself for living your life. For bringing Alonso down here. Your biggest strength isn't your brains,

Delaney. Though God knows you've got plenty. It's your heart."

She sniffed. "Don't be nice, Sam. Not now."

"I know. It'll ruin my image." He pressed his forehead to hers. "Guess I'll take the chance."

"I don't want to be alone tonight."

His brown eyes went black. A muscle suddenly ticked in his jaw. Then he lifted her, and her legs went around his hips as if they were designed much more for that purpose than any other.

"It doesn't change anything." Her voice was barely audible. The reminder was more for her than him.

But he'd heard, and his arms tightened around her. "I know that, too, Laney."

He carried her to his bedroom. With a single swipe, he yanked back the covers and settled her in the center of the bed. His gaze unwavering, he shrugged out of his shirt. Shucked the jeans.

Delaney watched, opening herself willingly to the heat he created, wanting it to coat the pain until she couldn't feel it anymore. "Hurry up."

But he wouldn't hurry. His expression gentled as he sat beside her and slowly slid his fingers beneath the straps of her dress. He drew them down until they fell loosely off her shoulders. Then his palms skimmed back up to her neck, to her face. And his mouth covered hers in an exquisitely slow kiss.

Her chest ached. Her eyes burned. She didn't want tenderness. She wanted blinding passion. Blessed forgetfulness. She dragged her hands down to his hips, pulling.

He caught her hands. Wove his fingers through them. Continued kissing her. Brushing his lips gently against hers.

A sob caught in her throat.

He didn't miss a beat. Brushing. Stroking. Never deepening or coaxing. Simply…kissing.

The sob birthed another. She struggled to keep it in.

His arm slid behind her. "Let it go, Laney. It's okay. Just let it go."

She looked at him through a glaze of tears.

And she finally let go. It was like opening a floodgate, and he held her all the while.

She cried for her father and she cried for Randy. She cried for the baby she'd lost, and she cried for the one that was probably only a wish.

Mostly she cried for the man and the marriage that she hadn't been able to keep.

And finally, when there were no more tears left, when she felt weak and spent and strangely cleansed, Sam still held her until she slept. But in the faint light of dawn, she woke again, only to find him awake, as well.

Still watching over her.

She lifted her hand, slowly outlining his lips. His lashes lowered for a moment, then his gaze met hers again, softened by the pale light slowly filling the room.

She sat up and pulled off her slept-in dress.

Sam lay there, still and watchful. Her dress rustled in the dawn hush as it fell from her outstretched fingers to the floor. For a moment, uncertainty held her in its grip. Then Sam lifted his hand and caught hers.

Threaded their fingers together, pressing his warm palm flush against hers. She closed her eyes for a moment, struggling to keep her equilibrium when need buffeted through her. His fingers tightened, inexorably drawing her toward him. Her body curved against him and her mouth found his.

He shifted, never releasing her hand, and caught the other, pressing them gently against the pillow beneath her head. And still he kissed her. The sheets rustled. She drew her foot along the heat of his calf, loving the feel of him. She dragged in a needful breath when his lips slid down to her jaw. Along her neck. Her shoulder. Words pushed at her throat, but wouldn't escape. She managed to whisper his name and he levered up, and looked at her. His heavy hair tumbled over his forehead. His eyes looked black in the golden glow slowly creeping across the room. He was completely masculine. Fierce with want. He was…Sam.

And even if she knew better, just then, he was hers.

She curled her fingers more tightly against his and bowed against him, catching her breath in tandem with his when she took him deep inside.

He held himself still for an eternity, his gaze searching hers. "Laney." He pressed his forehead against hers for a moment. Then caught her mouth with his.

And she was lost in the unbearable sweetness of loving her husband.

Diego made his run to the mainland early that morning so Delaney could catch the first flight out to New York.

"You want me to go with you?" Sam set her briefcase on the dock. Diego would throw down a ramp when the boat was ready.

"No. Thank you. I'm a big girl. I'll manage."

Back to politeness again. As if they hadn't spent the night together. She'd risen shortly after they'd made love. He'd listened to the water running in the shower. The faint sounds of her moving around in the guest bedroom. Packing up her briefcase. Doing whatever with the clothes she'd gotten since he'd forced her to stay on the island.

She hadn't come back to his bedroom, and he'd known the reprieve was over. Delaney Vega was back in control of all her faculties. She didn't need to lean on anyone.

Least of all her husband.

"You don't have to wait, if you've got things to attend to."

"Always thoughtful, Delaney." He leaned against the wood rail of the dock. The ocean smelled of salt and fish and wind. It blew over them, tossing her hair around her shoulders, plastering her thin floral skirt against her legs. "But I'll wait."

She lifted a shoulder as if to say "suit yourself." It irritated the hell out of him. He looked over to see what was taking Diego so long. The old man was tinkering with the motor, a greasy rag sticking out of his pocket.

The sight was too typical to worry him. He looked back at Delaney. "How'd Alonso take your leaving?" They'd stopped by Castillo House before coming to the dock.

"He knew I'd be going sooner or later."

Which was no answer at all. "What kind of strings did you have to pull to get him out of New York?"

She surprised him by even answering. "I threw around my mother's name and my father's reputation. How else do you think I could have managed it?"

He waited.

She sighed and shrugged. "I convinced Judge Wybrandt that he'd be better off here, and he wouldn't have to ever see Alonso's face in his courtroom again. One less orphaned teenager to deal with." She rubbed her hands down her arms against the chill in the early morning air. They could both hear Diego's muttered curses. An occasional clank of metal on metal. "How long is Diego going to take?"

"He has a time schedule all his own like everyone else on Turnabout. Don't worry. You'll catch your flight. You've got plenty of time yet."

"I wasn't worried."

"Right."

"You should make things up with your father," she said suddenly. "I know he's not perfect. But he's alive and he's well and he's here."

"And I make damn sure he follows the terms of his parole," he said bluntly, "so he can *stay* here."

Diego's banging grew louder. Then the engine turned. Misfired. The boat belched out a cloud of sickening exhaust. She coughed on the fumes. "I thought you were hard on him because of the past."

"The past. The future." He looked beyond her for a moment. "So he doesn't break Etta's heart."

She pressed her soft lips together for a moment. "And everyone thinks you're so hard."

"That's a good thing for a sheriff."

The small ferry chugged alongside the dock, then stopped. The wooden planks shuddered when Diego threw out a thick rope and hopped down. He flipped out the ramp. It thudded into place. "All set, Dr. Vega."

Delaney picked up her briefcase. She looked at Sam for a long moment. Then she stepped onto the boat.

Diego followed after her, tossing back the ramp. He scurried back to the engine room. The ferry rocked from side to side, water splashing up and over the edge of the dock, then began inching away.

Delaney leaned over the rail. "You asked me what I'd do if I could arrange my life to suit me." She had to raise her voice above the throb of the ferry.

"Yeah." It was the fumes from the boat getting to him, strangling his voice. He walked, keeping pace with the ferry.

"I'd arrange it so that everyone I loved would be happy."

His hands curled into fists. "Does that include me?" He'd dredged up the question from somewhere deep and dark.

She lowered her lashes for a moment. Then she looked at him. Even across the yards separating him, he could see them. Great pools of blue. Bottomless. "You married me before, out of obligation. I've known it all along. And I'm not pregnant now. There's no question anymore. No need to even take a test." Then she backed away from the rail, and the ferry picked up speed.

Sam's boots reached the end of the dock.

There was nowhere else to go.

He watched the boat chug away, until there was no sight of Delaney. No sight of the ferry at all.

He finally turned. Looked up the dock toward the island. Palm trees were bent back from the wind. The beach was blown smooth and white.

Feeling empty inside, he walked up the dock. No baby. No reason to convince her stay. With each fall of his boots on the wood, he heard the question again in his head. *Does that include me?*

He reached the end of the dock. Moved from wood planks to cement. From cement to a gravel lot.

Then his head snapped up and he peered out over the ocean.

Why hadn't she answered him?

He veered back to the shack housing Diego's quasi office. Snatched up the phone and dialed Castillo House. Spoke briefly with Logan.

Thirty minutes later he climbed aboard the chopper Logan had summoned and headed after her.

He needed to prove that some things would never change. And he needed to prove that some things *could*. So he didn't go alone.

Alonso went with him.

Chapter 16

By the time Delaney walked off the plane in New York, she felt disheveled and exhausted.

The ferry crossing had been windy, though Diego had been inordinately kind. He'd pressed hot coffee on her during the ride, checking on her regularly as if he feared she was going to bolt over the side of the boat. He even arranged the cab that took her from the ferry to the airport. When she'd tried to pay him, he'd waved away the money, assuring her that Sam had already taken care of the matter. After the crossing, where she'd had the ferry to herself, the flight in comparison had been cramped. She'd had to change planes, too, and the second leg hadn't been any better.

She followed along with the throng of people, trying

to close out the noise and the jostle that was distinctly jarring after the quiet of Turnabout. She veered off long enough to visit the restroom. Tried not to weep yet again the way she'd done in the shower that morning over the evidence that quashed the slim chance she and Sam had conceived another child.

She was nearly home, but there was no relief in it. And certainly no joy. Not with her father's funeral facing her. Not with the thought of facing Chad. There was no way she could pretend she'd be satisfied with common goals and interests without love, and continuing to practice with him would only be cruel to him.

She left the restroom and shuffled along with the crowd, her briefcase bumping against her hip. At least she didn't have luggage to retrieve. She'd left most of the items she'd purchased back at Sam's.

Thinking about *that* didn't help.

She fumbled with her cell phone, turning it on for the first time in days. It immediately began buzzing. She had messages waiting. She flipped the phone shut again and stuck it back in the side pocket of her briefcase. She'd listen to the messages later. On the taxi ride to her mother's place. It would help pass the time. Give her something to do.

Other than think.

"Looking for a ride?"

The low voice came toward her left ear and she jerked, whirling around, stopping dead in her tracks. But she hadn't hallucinated Sam's voice.

Her heart stopped. That was all. It just stopped. And when it started again, she felt dizzy.

She drank in the sight of him as if it had been days rather than hours since they'd parted. Blue jeans. Royal-blue shirt splotched with yellow and green. Sunglasses tucked in the collar of his shirt. And he stood right there in front of her, as solid as a boulder in a stream, the people passing by just flowing around him.

"How'd you get here?"

"We got a direct flight."

And then she noticed Alonso, standing several feet away. And she struggled to contain the fresh jolt of shock ripping through her. "You're not sending Alonso—"

"No."

She looked from the boy to Sam. "Then why?" She couldn't even articulate the rest of the question.

"We're going with you. I don't care that you think you don't need anyone. You shouldn't have to do this alone."

She glanced uneasily at the people brushing by them. "I'm sure my father would have appreciated you being there, but why bring—"

"Because we both love you."

Her lips parted, but nothing came out.

He smiled slightly and glanced back at Alonso, who stepped forward. Sam nudged her out of the flow of traffic into an empty gate area and pushed her down onto a molded seat. Then he sat beside her.

Alonso slumped down a few seats away, stretching out his long legs, trying to look disinterested. But his tennis shoe jiggled.

Then Sam touched her arm. And she looked back at him. His gaze burned over her face, and her heart began pounding. And he leaned forward and kissed her.

She forgot the announcements coming over the loud-speaker, the dull roar of footsteps and voices and cell phones ringing. She forgot everything but the feel of him. The taste of him.

Even as her fingers closed over his shoulders, twisting in the silky-thin fabric of his shirt, he was setting her away from him, leaving her breathless and feeling foolish. Alonso was watching them, looking vaguely fascinated by their display.

Sam shoved his hand through his hair, leaving the black strands spiked. "I didn't marry you because I felt sorry for you," he said abruptly.

She sucked down all her emotion. "What a comfort."

"Or only because you were pregnant. I married you because I fell in love with you the first day I met you. You were sitting across that bloody desk in your office with a superior little look on your beautiful face that basically told me I could go to hell before you'd forsake one of your clients to the case I was investigating."

She shifted, grateful to be sitting, because her legs were definitely shaky. That first meeting had been because of Alonso.

Sam's hooded gaze rested on her face. The bruise on his cheekbone seemed particularly prominent. "Probably should have just admitted that I loved you from the get-go. Maybe we wouldn't have made such a monumental mess of everything. Fact was—" he cocked his jaw for a moment "—the fact was you scared the hell out of me. You were completely out of my league. Smart enough to run circles around me."

"That's not true."

"But I wanted you more than I wanted air to breathe." Her throat tightened.

"And the second you lowered your defenses, I drove right on in, using the pregnancy as an excuse to get what I wanted. You were wrong when you said I was ashamed of our marriage." His voice went ragged. "But you were right when you said I didn't think it would last. Not even with the baby coming. Because the only reason you'd agreed to marry *me* was because you wanted our baby to have a father who cared about her."

She shook her head. "I never subscribed to the notion of someone's heart breaking."

"I know."

Her throat felt like a vise. "But I realized I was wrong when you walked out of our apartment."

"I'm sorry, Laney."

She exhaled shakily. "So now what? Nothing's changed. Even if we did contemplate…trying again, my chances of conceiving are slim at best—"

He moved swiftly out of his seat to crouch before her, his hands covering hers where they twisted together in her lap. "I wanted kids with *you*, Delaney. Nobody else. Because I loved you. I still love you. I will *always* love you. The question is, what do you want?"

"I want whatever will make you happy."

He caught her arms in his, shaking her gently. "What do *you* want, Delaney?" His voice was slow. Deliberate.

Tears clogged her nose. Her throat. *Sometimes love is all there is.* Etta's acerbic comment drifted through her mind. "You."

"Do you love me?"

How could one word be so hard to say? "Yes."

He exhaled as if he'd run a marathon. His head lowered to her lap, pressing against her hands. "Finally."

Her fingers flexed. Grazed the cool, thick silk of his hair. "How could you not know?"

He lifted his head. His eyes gleamed. "For the same reason you didn't. You never said the words. God, for two grown people, we've managed to make a royal mess of things." He sat back on his heels and pulled something from his pocket. Then he held out his hand.

She stared at the two wedding rings, her heart cracking wide open. Tears slid silently down her face and she didn't care. Not one little bit. "You kept your ring. I thought…I don't know. That maybe you'd heaved it off Luis's Point or something."

The corner of his mouth curled up. He handed her the larger ring but kept the smaller one. "I know I'm not going to get any awards for great timing here, but Delaney Townsend Vega," he said huskily, "I love you. And I need you. And I need you to admit that you need me, too. No more shutting each other out."

She didn't care about timing. "Sam." There was a knot in her throat. "I do need you. I always did." And admitting it wasn't nearly as hard as it was facing a future alone, without him.

He bent his head for a moment, then looked up again. His eyes were damp. "Then, will you come back to Turnabout with me and be my wife? Will you marry me?"

She dashed her hand across her cheek. "We're already married," she whispered.

"Oh, yeah, isn't that convenient." He kissed her palm. "Then, will you just come back to Turnabout and never think about leaving me again?"

She curled her fingers around the circle of his wedding ring. "Sam, why did you bring Alonso?"

He sat back again. Looked over at Alonso. The two eyed each other, then Alonso rolled his eyes and moved closer. "This is my cue, right?"

Sam nodded.

"What's going on between you two?"

"Sam thinks that maybe you, uh, you'd like us all to be a family."

Delaney sucked in her breath. She looked at Sam, hardly daring to believe it. "He does?"

"He does," Sam said. "I think we should petition for guardianship of Alonso."

She covered her mouth for moment. "You don't even like each other," she managed.

She saw the look Sam sent Alonso. And suddenly realized that they must have had some kind of meeting of the minds, in the time it had taken them to go from one coast to the other.

"I didn't like the fact that you gave your time so willingly to him when you wouldn't to me. Women don't have a corner on jealousy. But you love Alonso and I love you." A muscle in his jaw flexed. "And I know what it's like to have to live down a father's deeds. So maybe that's where our family is meant to begin."

Her heart squeezed. She looked up at the boy. "Alonso? What do you think about all this?"

He shrugged and dug the toe of his shoe harder against the corner of a cracked tile. "I told him he's out of his friggin' tree."

"Well," Delaney said faintly. "There's a surprise."

"But if it gets you to come back to Turnabout then I guess it's cool. Castillo House is okay, but it's hard to find a quiet place to read, you know? Still have to go there to shoot hoops, but…" He shrugged again.

"I don't want there to be a constant battle zone between you two," she said.

"We're not saying it'll be easy," Sam allowed. "But Alonso and I have agreed that there is one really big thing we have in common. We both love you. We'll probably keep each other on our toes for the next ten years making sure we live up to you."

Her head spun. Not in her wildest imaginings could she have anticipated, dreamed, hoped. "You two have this all figured out?"

Alonso nodded. He pushed his hands into his pockets. "I'll, uh, try not to disappoint you." He shot Sam a look. "Either one of you."

"There's only one point yet," Sam said.

"What could there possibly be left?"

"You have to say *yes,* V." Alonso shook his head, but he was finally smiling as he moved back to the seat several feet away.

And his smile took in *both* her and Sam.

"He's right." Sam turned to her again. "You have to say yes, Laney. We can have a ceremony all over again. No flying off to Vegas, though. No secrets. This one will have everyone there. Jessica if she'll come. Etta and Janie and Leo. Hell, I'll even allow Danté off his leash for the afternoon. He can't get in too much mischief as long as nobody gives him a pen. If you feel compelled, I can even tolerate Do-Wright for the event. Maybe Sara will like a tall blond guy who looks like Brad Pitt and it'll get Leo off his duff where she's concerned."

"Are you trying to bribe me?"

The corner of his mouth kicked up. His hands tightened around hers. "Is it working?"

She curled her fingers. "It'll take me a while to take care of the practice. I can't leave Chad in the lurch."

"I know. You wouldn't be you if you weren't doing back bends in order to be fair to everyone else. We can figure out details, Delaney. We've just got to figure out the important thing. To set our minds on what matters. And what matters is *us.*" His jaw cocked. "I know Turnabout is hardly a paradise. It's quiet and antiquated and—"

"And it's your home," Delaney leaned forward, cutting off his words with her fingers on his lips. "Though it hardly seemed quiet while I was there." His lips curved slightly beneath her fingertips. She swallowed. "It'll be our home. The first real one we'll have together."

He caught her hand in his, drawing it down. She realized there was a fine tremble in his tight grip. His thumbs slid over her wrists, pressing intimately against her frantically beating pulse. "Is that a yes?"

She nodded. "Yes. But I don't need another ceremony, Sam. Just put the ring on my finger. And I promise I'll never take it off again."

He slowly released her wrists. Lifted her hand and slid the ring home. Then he kissed it, exhaled and looked back at her. "I love you, Dr. Vega."

She lifted his hand and slid his ring back where it belonged. She lifted his hand, kissed it.

Then she looked into his eyes. The man she'd loved and nearly lost. And she saw something she'd always been afraid to believe in.

She saw forever.

"You can call me Mrs. Sam," she whispered, leaning forward into his kiss. "I like it better."

His mouth covered hers.

From somewhere she thought she heard Alonso mutter, "Finally."

Epilogue

The weather was postcard perfect for the middle of May. Blue skies, fluffy clouds and the faintest of breezes that blew through the palms. Even the air smelled fresh, lightly perfumed by the orange poppies that were springing up from nearly every inch of ground within the perimeter of the high iron fence surrounding Castillo House.

"It's a beautiful day for a wedding." Etta dabbed her eyes with a little kerchief.

Sam heard her and smiled. "Renewal of vows," he corrected for about the hundredth time. And the service was a lot later than they'd figured on. But once Delaney left New York and her practice there, she'd been busy settling into her new position at Castillo House, and they'd both been busy with the paperwork concerning Alonso's guardianship, which had finally been approved.

Etta just waved her hand at Sam, though, not concerned in the least with terminology. She sat forward in one of the white chairs that Logan, Sam and the kids of Castillo House had spent an hour setting out, which were now occupied by a good portion of Turnabout's population. "She *is* here, isn't she?"

Sam laughed. "Don't worry, Etta. She's here." Even though he hadn't seen her since early that morning, he knew exactly where Delaney would be. Exactly what she was doing. Their life together now was considerably different than it had been the first time around. Delaney had replaced Betty Weathers at Castillo House. He had agreed to take on some mayoral duties. But neither used their careers as an excuse to keep distance between them. Finally, they'd learned to work as a team.

"Relax, Etta." Danté stepped forward from his place with the groomsmen and urged Etta back into her seat, a grin hovering around his mouth. He'd been surprised when Sam asked him to stand up with him for the ceremony. Even after more than six months of Etta's Sunday dinners, there was still tension between Sam and his father. But it was getting better. And it would keep getting better.

"Well, I can't help it," she said. "I've waited a long time for this. The first wedding for one of my grandchildren." Her gaze cut to Sam warningly. If she wanted to call the ceremony a wedding, she was going to do just that. Then her expression softened again. "Just hope I don't have to wait as long for the next one." She eyed Leo, standing next to Sam.

He frowned and shook his head, looking as if bugs had been poured down his back. "Janie would be a better bet," Leo assured.

Etta exhaled noisily. "There's not a man on this island good enough for my Janie."

Since most of the Vega men agreed, they just grinned. Then the music began. A live harpist, courtesy of Delaney's mother who'd insisted on providing something for the ceremony.

Sam watched Jessica come down the aisle between the rows of chairs on the arm of Paolo, one of the newest boys to come to Castillo House. She sent a small smile their way as she sat in the front row across from Etta.

At least she had come. Had rearranged a trip to Europe by a few days in order to do so when Delaney had made a point of admitting how much she *wanted* Jessica to come. Do-Wright hadn't made it, though. Something about some conference he was speaking at. But he'd sent a telegram, and Delaney was happy.

Delaney.

He watched her walk from the house with the rest of her entourage. She stopped at the rear of the chairs, dwarfed by her young escort, while first April Fielding walked unerringly up the aisle, tossing out flower petals with abandon. She smiled brilliantly all the way. She'd been pretty happy about being the flower girl for Mrs. Sam, and had practiced walking the path until she'd perfected it.

When April got to the front, she slid into a chair next to Maisy and Caitlin, who'd returned to Castillo House with baby Zach.

Janie, Annie and Sara came next, followed by Rebecca Clay—an old friend of Delaney's who'd also left the city for small-town life. All the women looked lovely, too. But Sam barely noticed. He was busy watching his wife.

Then the harpist played a little louder, and Delaney started forward. The music wasn't a wedding march. She'd put her foot down about that. But it was bright and pretty, and when Sam glanced at Etta, he saw her toe tapping in time to it.

Then he looked back at his wife, and their gazes met, and he didn't see anything but her. She was beautiful. Hair pinned back. But that was okay, because he'd just get to unpin it later when they were alone. Her dress was a slip of a thing, thin layers of bluish-white fabric that swirled around her legs as she walked toward him. It made him think of the clouds drifting in the sky.

Then she stopped in front of him. And Alonso, who'd walked her down the aisle, moved over to stand beside Sam.

Delaney slanted them a look as she handed off her bouquet of flowers to Rebecca. He knew the flowers had come from Annie and Sara's fields. Just as the food being served at the reception afterward had come from Maisy, it seemed like everyone on Turnabout wanted to contribute to the event.

In the bare seconds before Sam moved beside Delaney, he nudged Alonso with his elbow. "Got the ring?"

Alonso shook his head, speaking under his breath. "Ah, man, Sam. You know what she's like. She wouldn't take it off. Said you'd given it to her once and that was all she needed."

Sam just smiled and took his place beside his wife. Her hand found his, which still wore his ring for the same reason, and their fingers linked tightly together.

The renewal of vows might be for them. But the ceremony was for everyone else who cared about them and was part of their lives.

They both looked over to Alonso, who was grinning as if he were personally responsible for arranging this more-than-perfect day. He didn't usually miss much opportunity these days to brag that he was the reason Delaney and Sam had ever met in the first place.

And that was okay.

The point was they had met, and they were finally on course the way they were meant to be.

And Sam didn't care that the pastor was still talking or that the service had barely even begun. He looked back down at the woman who'd filled his life with complications and challenges and love and a family that was more of a bonus than any man deserved. "I love you, Laney."

Her eyes went soft. "I love you, too, Samson."

Then he pulled her close and kissed her.

When he finally lifted his head, it was to laughter and cheers from the friends and family surrounding them. The pastor was eyeing them.

Delaney delicately touched the corner of her lip,

looking a little dazed. But then she spoke. And her voice was clear, so that everyone could hear.

"My husband marries me again. The least he can do is greet me with a kiss, wouldn't you all agree?"

* * * * *

Fall in Love with...

MEN
in UNIFORM

YES! Please send me the exciting *Men in Uniform* collection. This collection will begin with 3 FREE BOOKS and 2 FREE GIFTS in my very first shipment—and more valuable free gifts will follow! My books will arrive in 8 monthly shipments until I have the entire 51-book *Men in Uniform* collection. I will receive 2 free books in each shipment and I will pay just $4.49 U.S./$5.39 CDN for each of the other 4 books in each shipment, plus $2.99 for shipping and handling.* If I decide to keep the entire collection, I'll only have paid for 32 books because 19 books are free. I understand that accepting the 3 free books and gifts places me under no obligation to buy anything. I can always return a shipment and cancel at any time. My free books and gifts are mine to keep no matter what I decide.

263 HDK 2653   463 HDK 2653

Name	(PLEASE PRINT)	
Address		Apt. #
City	State/Prov.	Zip/Postal Code

Signature (if under 18, a parent or guardian must sign)

Mail to the **Harlequin Reader Service:**
IN U.S.A.: P.O. Box 1867, Buffalo, NY 14240-1867
IN CANADA: P.O. Box 609, Fort Erie, Ontario L2A 5X3

* Terms and prices subject to change without notice. Prices do not include applicable taxes. Sales tax applicable in N.Y. Canadian residents will be charged applicable taxes. This offer is limited to one order per household. All orders subject to approval. Credit or debit balances in a customer's account(s) may be offset by any other outstanding balance owed by or to the customer. Please allow 4–6 weeks for delivery. Offer available while quantities last. Offer not available to Quebec residents.

Your privacy: Harlequin is committed to protecting your privacy. Our Privacy Policy is available online at www.eHarlequin.com or upon request from the Reader Service. From time to time we may make our lists of customers available to reputable third parties who have a product or service of interest to you. If you would prefer we not share your name and address, please check here. ☐

MUBPA10

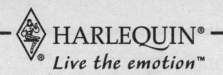

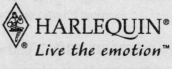

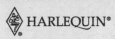

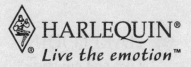

HARLEQUIN®
INTRIGUE®

BREATHTAKING ROMANTIC SUSPENSE

Shared dangers and passions lead to electrifying romance and heart-stopping suspense!

Every month, you'll meet six new heroes who are guaranteed to make your spine tingle and your pulse pound. With them you'll enter into the exciting world of Harlequin Intrigue— where your life is on the line and so is your heart!

THAT'S INTRIGUE— ROMANTIC SUSPENSE AT ITS BEST!

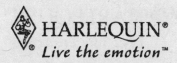

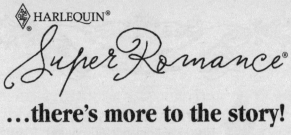

...there's more to the story!

Superromance.
A *big* satisfying read about unforgettable
characters. Each month we offer *six* very different
stories that range from family drama to adventure
and mystery, from highly emotional stories to
romantic comedies—and much more! Stories
about people you'll believe in and care about.
Stories too compelling to put down....

Our authors are among today's *best* romance
writers. You'll find familiar names and talented
newcomers. Many of them are award winners—
and you'll see why!

If you want the biggest and best
in romance fiction, you'll get it
from Superromance!

Exciting, Emotional, Unexpected...

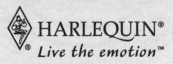

 **Harlequin® Historical**
Historical Romantic Adventure!

*Imagine a time of chivalrous
knights and unconventional ladies,
roguish rakes and impetuous
heiresses, rugged cowboys
and spirited frontierswomen—
these rich and vivid tales will
capture your imagination!*

*Harlequin Historical . . .
they're too good to miss!*